1

# HERSBAND MATERIAL 2: JAILHOUSE BUTCH

HERSBAND
MATERIAL
2

JAILHOUSE BUTCH

BY C. WASH

BY C. WASH

## Are You On Our Email List?

## Sign up on our website

## WWW.THECARTELPUBLICATIONS.COM

## Or text the word: CARTELBOOKS to 22828

## For prizes, contests, etc.

HERSBAND MATERIAL 2: JAILHOUSE BUTCH

## CHECK OUT OTHER TITLES BY THE CARTEL PUBLICATIONS

SHYT LIST 1: BE CAREFUL WHO YOU CROSS
SHYT LIST 2: LOOSE CANNON
SHYT LIST 3: AND A CHILD SHALL LEAVE THEM
SHYT LIST 4: CHILDREN OF THE WRONGED
SHYT LIST 5: SMOKIN' CRAZIES THE FINALE'
PITBULLS IN A SKIRT 1
PITBULLS IN A SKIRT 2
PITBULLS IN A SKIRT 3: THE RISE OF LIL C
PITBULLS IN A SKIRT 4: KILLER KLAN
PITBULLS IN A SKIRT 5: THE FALL FROM GRACE
POISON 1
POISON 2
VICTORIA'S SECRET
HELL RAZOR HONEYS 1
HELL RAZOR HONEYS 2
BLACK AND UGLY
BLACK AND UGLY AS EVER
MISS WAYNE & THE QUEENS OF DC
BLACK AND THE UGLIEST
A HUSTLER'S SON
A HUSTLER'S SON 2
THE FACE THAT LAUNCHED A THOUSAND BULLETS
YEAR OF THE CRACKMOM
THE UNUSUAL SUSPECTS
LA FAMILIA DIVIDED
RAUNCHY
RAUNCHY 2: MAD'S LOVE
RAUNCHY 3: JAYDEN'S PASSION
MAD MAXXX: CHILDREN OF THE CATACOMBS (EXTRA RAUNCHY)
KALI: RAUNCHY RELIVED: THE MILLER FAMILY
REVERSED
QUITA'S DAYSCARE CENTER
QUITA'S DAYSCARE CENTER 2
DEAD HEADS
DRUNK & HOT GIRLS
PRETTY KINGS
PRETTY KINGS 2: SCARLETT'S FEVER
PRETTY KINGS 3: DENIM'S BLUES
PRETTY KINGS 4: RACE'S RAGE
HERSBAND MATERIAL
UPSCALE KITTENS
WAKE & BAKE BOYS
YOUNG & DUMB
YOUNG & DUMB: VYCE'S GETBACK
TRANNY 911
TRANNY 911: DIXIE'S RISE
FIRST COMES LOVE, THEN COMES MURDER
LUXURY TAX
THE LYING KING
CRAZY KIND OF LOVE
SILENCE OF THE NINE

## BY C. WASH

SILENCE OF THE NINE II: LET THERE BE BLOOD
SILENCE OF THE NINE III
PRISON THRONE
GOON
HOETIC JUSTICE
AND THEY CALL ME GOD
THE UNGRATEFUL BASTARDS
LIPSTICK DOM
A SCHOOL OF DOLLS
SKEEZERS
SKEEZERS 2
YOU KISSED ME NOW I OWN YOU
NEFARIOUS
REDBONE 3: THE RISE OF THE FOLD
THE FOLD
CLOWN NIGGAS
THE ONE YOU SHOULDN'T TRUST
COLD AS ICE
THE WHORE THE WIND BLEW MY WAY
SHE BRINGS THE WORST KIND
THE HOUSE THAT CRACK BUILT
THE HOUSE THAT CRACK BUILT 2: RUSSO & AMINA
THE HOUSE THAT CRACK BUILT 3: REGGIE & TAMIKA
THE HOUSE THAT CRACK BUILT 4: REGGIE & AMINA
LEVEL UP
VILLAINS: IT'S SAVAGE SEASON
GAY FOR MY BAE
WAR
WAR 2
WAR 3
WAR 4
WAR 5
WAR 6
WAR 7
MADJESTY VS. JAYDEN
YOU LEFT ME NO CHOICE
TRUCE: A WAR SAGA (WAR 8)
TRUCE 2: THE WAR OF THE LOU'S (WAR 9)
AN ACE AND WALID VERY, VERY BAD CHRISTMAS (WAR 10)
TRUCE 3: SINS OF THE FATHERS (WAR 11)
TRUCE 4: THE FINALE (WAR 12)
ASK THE STREETS FOR MERCY
TREASON
TREASON 2
HERSBAND MATERIAL 2
THE END. HOW TO WRITE A BESTSELLING NOVEL IN 30 DAYS

**WWW.THECARTELPUBLICATIONS.COM**

5

**HERSBAND MATERIAL 2: JAILHOUSE BUTCH**

# HERSBAND

# MATERIAL 2:

# JAILHOUSE BUTCH

# BY

# C. WASH

HERSBAND MATERIAL 2: JAILHOUSE BUTCH
BY C. WASH

HERSBAND MATERIAL 2: JAILHOUSE BUTCH

PUBLISHER'S NOTE:
This book is a work of fiction. Names,
characters, businesses,
Organizations, places, events and
incidents are the product of the
Author's imagination or are used
fictionally. Any resemblance of
Actual persons, living or dead, events, or
locales are entirely coincidental.

Library of Congress Control Number: 2013931063

ISBN 10: 0996099239

ISBN 13: 978-0996099233

Cover Design: Davida Baldwin Odd Ball
Designs

First Edition

Printed in the United States of America

BY C. WASH

What's Good Twisted Babies & Friends!

First let me start by saying, BRAVO, Baby!

I saw you battle whether or not to follow up on your first novel. And I watched you go through the many roads you'd need to travel to bring Mystro and Native back to fruition. It wasn't easy because you do so much for me, Cece and The Cartel Publications, that life for you is busy.

You are literally the glue and the love that keeps our family together. And yet you decided to add to your schedule writing a book?

But guess what, baby?

You nailed it!

Through the words on your pages, I saw Mystro, Native and Baby Dom again as if they were long lost family members. I watched the turmoil they went through in many attempts to find their paths.

And I held my breath wondering if they would make decisions that would change their

9

lives and the lives of people around them for the worse. Readers will thoroughly enjoy this follow up because it has everything the original held and more!

Enjoy Cartel Publications Family!

Let's gooooo!!!

Give the VP some love!

With that being said, keeping in line with tradition, we want to give respect to a vet, new trailblazer paving the way or pay homage to a favorite. In this novel, we would like to recognize:

# THE PROLIFIC PENS

These up-and-coming national bestselling authors decided to write a book together after being members of our tribe. With focus, determination, and love for collaboration, they inspired me, our tribe and so many others.

Congratulations, Prolific Pens!

BY C. WASH

We love you!

T. STYLES

PRESIDENT & CEO

The Cartel Publications

**www.thecartelpublications.com**

Instagram: authortstyles

Instagram: Publishercwash

**www.twitter.com/cartelbooks**

**www.facebook.com/cartelpublications**

www.theelitewritersacademy.com

Follow us on Instagram: Cartelpublications

**#CartelPublications**

**#UrbanFiction**

**#PrayForCece**

**#Theprolificpens**

# DEDICATION

I dedicate this novel to **TWO** of my favorite people:

**FIRST**: My beautiful, talented, and creative wife! **TOY**, I have no idea where I would be without you, and I thank God that I'm so blessed to have you in my life. I appreciate how much you ALWAYS believe in me and show me that ANYTHING is possible. I love you to the moon and back, baby! Thank you.

**SECOND**: My sister **CECE "SEVEN" WASHINGTON**. You are my absolute hero my nig! Every move I make is with you in mind. I will ALWAYS have your back and if need be, your front. Eye of the tiger, champ! You are making amazing strides and I can't wait until you get back on the stage where you belong ;)
I love your crazy ass!

– **RISSE**

**BY C. WASH**

# HERSBAND MATERIAL 2: JAILHOUSE BUTCH

# #HERSBANDMATERIAL2

BY C. WASH

# PROLOGUE

The room was stuffy and hot.

Only the sounds of dripping water could be heard. The other sound was deep breathing and an elevated heartbeat.

Everything happened so fast.

But if she could go back and do it over again what would be different?

As she stood there trying to get a solid rhythm in her breath, in her heart, she contemplated what was her next step.

Standing over the body she needed a plan and she needed one now.

If she ran, there was no guarantee someone wouldn't see her. In her condition she was sure they wouldn't understand. But if she stayed, how would she get out of this?

She needed a miracle.

While realizing that she was undeserving.

"What the fuck am I gonna do now?" She said out loud to herself.

15

The only thing she could think to do at the moment, pray.

"God, you know my heart. You know I didn't mean for things to go this way. If you see fit to get me out of this predicament, I will never be put in it again. Amen."

Before she could complete making the sign of the cross over her chest, the door opened.

She swallowed the lump that bulged in her throat.

Who she saw next made her heart skip ten beats faster, making her feel close to death.

**BY C. WASH**

# CHAPTER ONE
# MYSTRO
## 3 MONTHS EARLIER

Mystro placed both hands on each one of Breezy's ass cheeks as she licked around her asshole like an ice cream cone. Her stomach lay flat on the bed with her ass high in the air as Mystro went to work.

Breezy was so turned on her pussy dripped in anticipation. It felt better than amazing, and she wished the moment lasted forever.

Mystro decided to stop teasing her and fully engulfed her clit. She sucked it hard and then softer from the back which sent chills all over Breezy's body. When she let out a moan, Mystro knew she was on the verge of cumming.

"Turn that ass over." Mystro instructed as Breezy obeyed. This was her playground and she was in complete control.

17

Feeling the moment, Breezy turned onto her back with her legs spread open.

The perfect view.

Mystro took in her body first before she made a move. She certainly looked good enough to eat. She looked down into Breezy's eyes and then, when she was ready, lowered her head.

Breezy grabbed her ankles and anticipated feeling Mystro's tongue again.

She didn't disappoint.

Mystro placed her warm mouth over her pussy and softly licked her clit. Breezy's body heated up and she knew her orgasm was quickly approaching.

Mystro knew it too.

She could feel her body vibrating.

Suddenly, without warning, Mystro placed her right hand up around Breezy's throat and began to squeeze. As she choked her neck, she stiffened her tongue and sucked her clit to ensure that she would cum hard.

Breezy was in ecstasy.

On the brink of her nut, Breezy moaned and gripped Mystro's braids.

Mystro didn't stop.

She continued her oral attack until she felt Breezy's cum saturate her tongue.

In between the tongue flips, she looked up to catch Breezy's face because she loved how she bit down on her lip when she came hard. But instead of Breezy, she saw her ex-girlfriend Church's face.

Mystro jumped up frightened, not knowing what was happening.

There was a devious look in her eyes. Church lay there and motioned with her index finger for Mystro to come back and finish.

Mystro shook her head to try and make Church disappear.

She didn't.

Instead, Church started laughing and playing with her pussy.

Mystro was having an out of body experience. Slowly she backed up and looked around the room and noticed a body lying on the floor.

Where was she?

What was happening?

She slowly approached it.

When she stood over top of the body, she was looking down at Breezy's face who appeared to be dead. She had blood coming from a bullet wound in her chest. And looked grayed over.

Mystro fell forward and grabbed Breezy's face before letting out a loud scream.

When she felt her heart trip, as her mind returned to reality, she jumped up out of bed.

She was having a nightmare.

Relieved, she flopped back down on the bed and fell onto her back. She was trying to catch her breath while she wiped the sweat from her forehead and neck.

As Mystro tried to calm herself, she ran her hand through her short curly hair and observed her surroundings.

Her eyes rolled all over her cell before they settled on her celly's bunk above her. Reality hit hard. She remembered exactly where she was, still in prison for killing her cheating ex-girlfriend.

Almost a year ago, Mystro walked in on her ex, Church, while she fucked her boyfriend in Mystro's apartment. She shot her and for that crime she was locked up.

Her world destroyed.

While still trying to gather herself, Mystro smelled the foul scent of her cellmate, Logan's, fart that seemed to take over the tiny space.

She put her t-shirt over her nose and got out of her bunk. Slowly, she walked over to the mirror attached to the sink and stared at her reflection.

Her eyes roamed over her face and down to the tattoo on her chest. She shook her head at the fact that it displayed Church's name surrounded by angels wings and realized how it looked like a remembrance tat. Why hadn't she noticed that before now.

She shook her head and decided that the first chance she got, she would have it covered up. She didn't need any more reminders of that broad.

"Never again." Mystro said to herself softly while she looked in the mirror.

"You the one let a hoe get in your head and get you fucked up." Logan said groggily to her from her bunk. She swung her long red braids out of her face.

Logan was a white girl who shared Mystro's cell. She was short and thick with a huge personality.

Mystro focused on her. "Slim, I ain't ask for your opinion. And what the fuck you been eating? You got our whole house smelling like chitterlings."

Logan laughed and ignored her comment. Because she wasn't about to hold her gas for no one. "I told you these bitches ain't shit! If you keep letting them, they will fuck your head up every time."

"Leave it, Lo."

"Let me ask you something, how come you never try to have fun? I mean I know we up in this bitch locked up, but you gotta make the best of this shit."

"Logan, we ain't at summer camp and I ain't here for all that. The only thing I'm focused on is my appeal. I'm trying to get out of here and regain a sense of peace. In the meantime, I'm doing what's in front of me and keeping my head down."

"But I'm–."

"Fun ain't in the equation for me." Mystro schooled. "Ain't nothing about my circumstance or life fun."

"My, that time will be a lot harder and a lot longer if you don't find a way to get through it."

Mystro looked down.

**23**

"You know I can get my hands on whatever you need so take advantage." Logan continued. "Nothing is too big or too small. If you want McDonald's, I got you. I know you like books, I can get 'em, but figure out something. Trust me, you're gonna need it."

Mystro took a brief pause and chose her words carefully. "I appreciate the advice; I really do but don't worry 'bout me. I'm gucci."

"That'll be a little harder, but I can get you that too." Logan laughed.

Mystro shook her head.

Suddenly, they heard a loud buzzing sound and the cell door popped unlocked and a guard pushed the door open.

"Mason, it's time to head out." C.O. Michael said as he stepped inside the cell.

"Okay, here I come." Mystro grabbed her toiletries and bath towel and headed out the door with the guard.

"I meant to tell you, I like the haircut. Looks good on you. My wife wants to cut her hair but I'm not with it. No way is she gonna walk

24

around looking like no dyke." C.O. Michael stated before he cut his eyes to Mystro. "No offense."

Mystro didn't say anything as the two continued to walk down the quiet hallway.

She was certainly a Dom of few words.

It was early in the morning and all the inmates were still locked in their cells.

Mystro worked in the kitchen, and she had to prep the food before chow time. Although Mystro dreamed of being a chef, cooking for hundreds of prisoners was not what she had in mind.

She made a mental note the next time she envisioned her goals in life she had to be more specific.

"I really didn't mean anything by that, Mason. My fault." C.O. Michael continued feeling bad about his comment.

"Nah, it's cool." She said with furrowed eyebrows.

"Uh, so what's on the menu for this morning?" He asked, placing a hand on his protruding stomach.

"Same old shit, powdered eggs, frozen potatoes, breakfast meat, and toast. I'll be so glad when we get the new kitchen order so I can add some variety."

"Oh nah, from what I've seen you do, you know how to whip up fire from scraps. Some of the meals you come up with in here taste better than shit I get on the outside." C.O. Michael confessed.

"Thank you, man. I really appreciate that."

"No problem. So, where'd you learn to cook that good?" He asked as they continued to the destination.

"I had a dream of being a chef. But when I landed in here, it appeared that my dream would never come true. It's real funny how things come to fruition, especially when you have time on your hands, literally."

C.O. Michael chuckled.

"I never got a chance to go to culinary school, but I spent hours looking up classes and taught myself a lot."

"Yeah, but to run the kitchen here I know you needed experience so how'd you swing it?"

"You right, the warden wasn't trying to let me cook at all, but I begged him to let me whip up something for a taste test and after a few no's, he let me in the kitchen." Mystro said happily.

"Oh, ok. I did hear about a meal you cooked up for him when I started working here. Your legend preceded you." He confessed.

"Yep! I knew I only had one shot, so I hit the kitchen and immediately rushed the pantry and refrigerator to see what I had to work with. I grabbed several items and when my raid was over, I had whipped up Shrimp Alfredo Pasta with garlic bread."

"Bullshit, Mystro." C.O. Michael said as he laughed. "You made that with the shit in this kitchen?" He pointed out in front of them.

Mystro became sullen, as she thought about the time before that when she last made the dish for Church in the apartment they shared together.

C.O. Michael noticed her sudden mood change. "Come on, man tell me, how'd you make that type of dish here?"

Mystro wiped her hand down her face and continued. "Uh well, since it's prison, I had to make my alfredo sauce from scratch using canned milk, butter, garlic salt and parmesan cheese. I used spaghetti noodles that were in the pantry and my shrimp had to come out of a can from commissary. I got peppers to add from a frozen bag of mixed veggies. Instead of having a fresh garlic baguette, I had to toast white sandwich bread, added melted butter and sprinkled garlic salt over it."

"Damn!" C.O. Michael stated. "Where was I?" He chuckled.

"After he ate that, the job was mine." Mystro said with zero enthusiasm.

"Well, I know I'm impressed. I would love to see how you come up with my favorite meal." He said dry begging.

"Just tell me what it is and I'll do what I can." Mystro stated.

C.O. Michael smiled, "Ok, we'll see."

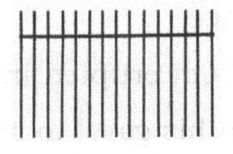

Showered and dressed in fresh prison whites, Mystro walked to the door to look out into the cafeteria. She was different now, no longer the *sucker for love ass lesbian* she had been before. She just wanted to do her time, cook and work towards getting out.

Truthfully, the only thing that brought a smile to her face these days was being able to cook.

She reflected on the events that led her to where she stood presently.

HERSBAND MATERIAL 2: JAILHOUSE BUTCH

Her thoughts periodically moved to the past, and now was no different.

She was in a semi-crowded courtroom standing and waiting for the verdict to be read when her friend, who she and her best friend, Native affectionately nicknamed, Baby Dom, stood up and blurted out that she killed Grover Lawrence.

The courtroom erupted in a roar as Judge Tredall banged his gavel to regain order. After court quieted down, he instructed the bailiff to remand Baby Dom to the holding cell and called for a brief recess.

After the outbreak and newfound revelation, the judge ordered a retrial.

Mystro had to go through the whole thing all over again, but this time, minus the charge of Grover's murder.

She was convicted of second-degree murder for the killing of Church Oliver and was sentenced to ten years with parole eligibility after five.

Mystro shook the past away and looked out at the food service line of inmates, the last thing she wanted to be doing in prison was not be paying attention. One thing Logan told her when she first got there was to watch her surroundings, always.

When she looked up from the line and back out into the hallway, she saw wall to wall inmates, but it was one, in particular, that snatched the breath out of Mystro's lungs.

And although they went way back, she lowered her head and pretended they did not.

# CHAPTER TWO
# NATIVE

**N**ative took the steps that led to her apartment two at a time with ease. She slid her hand into her cargo pants pocket to grab her keys. Once she located them, she singled out the one she needed and stuck it in the lock.

As she walked through her doorframe she was greeted by the sexy sight of her live-in girlfriend, Brisa.

Native smiled wide.

Brisa stood in the middle of the living room wearing a red bustier and matching thong, garters, black fishnet leggings and black stilettos. Although her body said sex, her glare screamed pissed.

"Now why is that beautiful face twisted up?" Native joked as she took off her leather jacket and readjusted her two long French braids down her back.

"Don't start with me! You got off work over two hours ago! Where have you been, Native?" Brisa came straight for her head. "And don't fucking lie either."

Native laughed Brisa out like she was joking, but Brisa didn't crack a smile.

"Bri, you serious?" Native questioned not moving in anticipation of her answer.

Brisa didn't utter a word, just continued to give Native the death stare.

"Baby, I stopped at Floormart to grab a HDMI cord so we can watch our favorite web series, *Bmore Chicks* on the TV instead of the laptop." She held the bag containing the cord up as proof.

"Don't give me that shit, Native," she yelled, waving the air. "Floormart is up the street, that little trip would only account for thirty minutes to just get a damn cord. You think I'm stupid, don't you?"

"Bri—"

"Don't Bri me! I told you if we moved in together, I wouldn't be made a fool of, Native. I can't be." Brisa yelled before she stormed off into the kitchen. "Not again!"

Native stood in the living room stuck.

The old Native would normally chuck up the deuces and dip on her. Leaving Brisa not only feeling stupid but looking stupid for a perfect match. Native was the love 'em and leave 'em strung out type of lesbian.

But not with this one.

Shit had to be different.

Native met Brisa over a year ago while she and her best friend Mystro were in PG Plaza parking lot staking out on a caper to rob people. The caper was an attempt to get money after being fired from their job.

And then she saw her face.

Brisa came out of the mall and Native couldn't resist her.

She hopped out the car not even telling her partner Mystro what was going on and ran up

34

to Brisa before she got away. She got her attention with a dry ass line and without a whole lot of effort on Native's part, she walked away with Brisa's number. She never got the chance to call Brisa before she ran into her again at the most unlikely place, her hotel room.

Back in the day Mystro and Native were everywhere.

They took to being hired for escort services after their brief stint as exotic dancers to remain gainfully employed. They were under the direction of Mystro's ex-girl, Church. This meant they went on paid dates and one of their dates was for a private party.

When they arrived, they were greeted by Brisa and Breezy, Mystro's friend and hair stylist, who had hired them both for the evening. Brisa and Native hit it off and had been inseparable ever since.

After Mystro's arrest and trials, Brisa was there for Native. After all, Native lost her best friend to the system. And it was Brisa who stepped into the right-hand position.

They got so close they decided to move in together. That meant that Native would have to find a good job and move out of the house she stayed in with her mother, Margaret.

She found a job at Horizon Cell Phone Company, although she hated every minute of it. But, it was a steady income so they looked for apartments.

Prior to cohabitating, Brisa and Native's relationship was great, but somehow as the boxes were moved into their new spot, so were Brisa's insecurities. Native found herself constantly reassuring Brisa that she was being faithful and today was no different.

Instead of reverting to her old ways which meant leaving out and finding something sexy, and warm to be with temporarily, Native slid off into the bathroom and took a quick shower.

When she reemerged, she had on only a navy-blue Polo robe, boxer briefs, a sports bra and Washington Nationals socks.

36

Her many tattoos on full display all over her mocha-colored skin.

As she approached the front of the apartment where Brisa was, Native pulled out her cell phone and looked for a specific song. Satisfied, she took a deep breath. She hit the symbol in her playlist to hear, *"How Do I Say"* by Usher.

The opening of the song came booming out of the Bluetooth speaker in the dining room.

Brisa was on the couch in the adjacent living room. She flipped through channels on the TV and tried to ignore Native, but she was having none of it.

Native moved slowly to the music with only one thing on her mind...seduction.

♪♫ *A foreign beauty so exotic* ♪♫
*When she smiled at me*
*She took my breath away.*
*She's reminiscent of a goddess*

Native reached inside her robe pocket and pulled out a small bottle of baby oil. She squirted some into the palm of her hand and tossed the bottle onto a chair in the living room.

She rubbed the oil all over her stomach in a silly fashion trying to be over the top.

Brisa put her hand up to her mouth to hide her laugh as she took her eyes off the TV and onto the live show before her.

"What you doing?" Brisa asked with a smirk although she could low-key not resist.

Native didn't utter a word, just continued her routine.

She dropped her robe to the floor and allowed Brisa to take in her body fully.

She used the opportunity to flex her lubed up ab muscles and played right into the hands of Brisa who was no longer laughing and appeared to be turned on the more Native moved.

She slowly approached Brisa.

Even closer.

She stood over her and took in the view.

Brisa looked up into Native's eyes with ecstasy.

Her pussy tingled in anticipation of the fuck session that seemed to be nearing.

Reducing her height, Native got on her knees in front of Brisa and pushed her legs open.

Brisa was all in, ready to take the trip to wherever Native wanted them to go.

Native reached behind Brisa's back and snatched at her thong to get it off her.

Brisa lifted her ass up to allow it to come off easier. In other words, she was willing to help.

When Native got it off, she tossed it to the floor and ran her middle and index fingers down Brisa's clit and into her soaked pussy.

Brisa inhaled deeply and threw her head back.

Native licked her fingers and said, "Mmmmmmm."

Brisa licked her lips.

Native reached around Brisa's back and this time cupped her ass cheeks and pulled Brisa forward so that she was face to pussy.

She went in.

She covered Brisa's whole clit with her mouth and proceeded to devour it.

Brisa began to moan loudly.

As Native attempted to lick and suck Brisa into a coma, Brisa tried to squirm away from her grasp but couldn't move.

Native had her on lock and knew it was only a matter of time before she came.

"Native, please, please don't stop." She said softly as she whined.

Native gripped her ass harder and put her tongue in turbo and it was curtains.

"Ohhhhhhhh, ohhhhhhhhh, Native, mmmmmmmmmmm." She screamed out.

40

Native shifted her tongue out of turbo and started to suck deeply to ensure Brisa had nothing left.

When she knew her work was done and Brisa was lying back trying to catch her breath, Native got up and said, "Come with me."

She was just getting started.

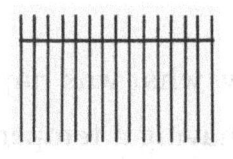

"Bae, what time you plan on getting up?" Brisa asked as she lay on her left side toward Native. They had just gotten up from their slumber after back-to-back love making sessions all night.

"In a minute," Native replied. "Then I'ma slide through mom's crib to check on the 'ole bird. Why, what you doing today?" Native responded.

Brisa didn't say a word. Instead, she turned her body away from Native onto her back and crossed her arms over her chest in anger.

What just happened? "I know you ain't pouting?" Native teased.

Brisa didn't move.

"What, shawty?" Native shot.

"Nothing," Brisa said as she jumped up from the bed and headed toward the bathroom.

Native knew what was happening.

Brisa was having a temper tantrum.

Once again.

Every time she didn't get her way she got pissed and shut down. Native had no clue why she had her chest puffed out at the moment, but wasn't in the mood to stroke Brisa's ego either.

On the flipside, she also knew that if she didn't address this attitude now, it would only get worse later.

Against her better judgment, Native threw the black flannel sheet off her, and shot out the bed.

"Damn," Native sighed and put her head down as she trudged toward the bathroom. It was the last thing she felt like dealing with, especially after all the work she put in last night.

Before she knocked, she stared at the bathroom door and took a deep breath. She needed to get herself in a calm head space before she went in, or her words would come out wicked.

KNOCK KNOCK KNOCK.

"I'm in here." Brisa yelled.

"I know, can I come in?" Native asked, although she didn't feel like the morning drama.

Silence.

Native turned the gold doorknob slowly. As the door creaked open, she hung in the doorway.

Brisa stood at the sink as she angrily brushed her teeth.

"B, what's up, why you beefing with me? 'Cuz I said I'm going to mom's?" Native asked softly.

"Oh, I'm not tripping, what makes you think I am?" She mumbled.

"Cuz you stomped in here and are brushing your teeth so mean your gums bleeding." Native replied.

Brisa rolled her eyes and stopped her tooth attack. "Whatever. I'm not tripping off of shit." She turned the water on and rinsed her toothbrush.

"Talk to me, Bri." Native pleaded.

"You didn't even think about me or even find out what I'm doing. I had to ask you first. It's like you don't wanna spend no time with me."

"Shawty, what you mean? We live together. How is that not spending time with you?" Native replied with shoulders and arms raised towards the ceiling.

"Hold up, you think just because we live together that means we spend time with each other?" Brisa asked.

"You don't?" Native questioned seriously.

"What am I even doing here with you? You don't give a fuck about me or this relationship, do you?"

"Shawty--"

"Stop calling me that shit!" Brisa demanded. "I ain't one of your groupie bitches whose name you can't remember." She slapped at her chest so hard it reddened. "My name is Brisa! Call me that or don't talk to me!"

Native stood dumbfounded.

She could not believe that the girl she fell in love with a year ago was standing in the bathroom in the apartment they shared going on her with toothpaste around her lips like a mad dog foaming at the mouth.

What's worse was, she still didn't really understand why she had an attitude.

45

Native was slowly reaching the end of her rope with Brisa.

She would have never agreed to move in with her if she knew she was gonna start unbelievably lunching.

The bathroom makeup attempt failed.

She tried.

But how much petty shit did she really feel like dealing with? She began to sense her blood boil under her skin and decided that enough was enough.

No Mas!

"Fuck!" Native yelled. "What is your problem, slim? I'm doing all I can to treat you with respect and be considerate towards you but all you do is drive me the fuck crazy!" Native continued.

"Who do you think you-"

"Nah, who the fuck you think you talking too?" Native shot back, cutting Brisa off and answering her question at the same time. "I'm not a mind reader. So either say what your attitude is about or huff and puff this whole apartment down by yourself, shit!"

Brisa was floored.

Never had Native talked to her so harshly before. She was at a loss for words.

"You act like I don't have reason to feel the way I do, Native. Did you forget that you are the one who runs through bitches like draws?" Brisa explained.

Native took a deep breath. "It ain't even–"

"I'm asking a question!"

When she cut her off it always irritated Native. It was bad enough trying to apologize for some shit she didn't do. But to be cut off at the same time drove her insane.

She took a deep breath. "Bri, when have you ever caught me out there fucking around on you? I'll answer that...Never." Native yelled, stomping her foot into the cold bathroom floor.

"Just because I haven't caught you doesn't mean it hasn't happened." Brisa said with tears that welled up in her eyes.

Native inhaled and exhaled loudly.

The woman was obviously used to women treating her like shit. And although that was Native's brand, she was trying.

Trying to be the better version of herself.

Trying to show Brisa that she was in her corner.

So, she stepped into the bathroom fully and grabbed Brisa's face cloth off the towel rack.

"I'm doing right by you but you gotta give a nigga some space." She wiped the toothpaste from her mouth. "I can't keep living like this." Native stared at Brisa and waited for her reaction.

Truth be told she would have loved it if Brisa gave her back her flying card so she could leave the relationship without malice, guilt or an afterthought, but she knew that was a long shot. Especially since it was true that Native hadn't really done anything for Brisa to want her gone.

Brisa sat in Native's words.

"Ok," Brisa stated. "I'm sorry, you right...you haven't done anything that I have the right to be going on you about so, truce?" She asked.

Native smiled. "Truce."

"I really just wanted you to go with me to the mall today and grab a gift for Carol's baby shower." Brisa confessed.

Native shook her head. "Damn, Bri. We went through all this arguing and bullshit for nothing. Next time just fast forward to this part." Native demanded. "Yeah, I'll roll with you."

Brisa now displayed a huge smile on her face and wanted to really show Native how happy she was that she decided to go with her.

She took Native's hand and guided her in front of the toilet. She pushed her gently down on top of the closed lid.

Although the seat was ice cold on the back of Native's thighs, she took it like a champ as she deduced that soon enough, she'd be warm all over.

Brisa went to work.

She removed Native's boxer briefs and got on her knees in between Native's legs. Slowly but with focus, she parted Native's pussy lips that exposed her clit and covered it with her mouth. Native took a deep breath and threw her head back loving how Brisa was remitting the gift of head she'd given her the night before.

Brisa went in bobbing her head back and forth as she licked and sucked Native with precision.

She knew just how much Native loved it like that. Besides, she'd done this many times before.

The coolness of Brisa's minty fresh tongue almost took Native out. It was so good that within three minutes, Native exploded onto Brisa's tongue.

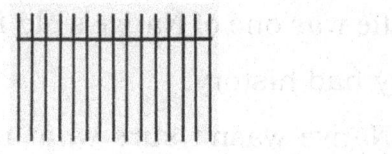

Native and Brisa walked out of Lacy's department store, with a shopping bag carrying a baby shower gift. They were headed to BTLR shoe store so Native could cop a pair of New Balance 992's.

Although it was fall and heading fast towards winter, you wouldn't catch Native without her gray New Balance's on unless there was at least three inches of snow outside.

As they walked down the semi crowded mall Native, slowed her pace when she looked out ahead.

Out of all the faces she saw, she couldn't believe who was walking toward her and Brisa's direction.

Ife.

Ife was one of Native's old fuck buddies and they had history.

Native wasn't sure what to do. She hadn't seen or spoken to Ife in a long time, so she wasn't cheating on Brisa with her. But still, the situation was awkward.

What would Ife say?

What would Brisa do?

Native decided she didn't want to find out.

She pulled her red Washington Wizards cap down low over her two French braids that came down toward the middle of her back. She aimed to keep her head down in an attempt to pretend she didn't see Ife.

But Ife peeped them ten minutes ago and was ready to blow shit up per usual.

"Native", Ife said as she paused directly in front of her and Brisa.

Native was about to do a walk by.

"Please stop playing 'cuz I know you see me." Ife continued.

"Oh...hey, what up, Ife?" Native responded nervously.

Fuck! It didn't work.

Native raised her cap to the right position.

"I was fine until I saw you about to walk by."

"It wasn't even like that." Native lied.

"Well, how you been, boo?" Ife asked.

"Boo?" Brisa questioned. Truthfully, she was waiting on introductions but Native had failed. "I know you see me standing here, whore." Brisa continued as she shot daggers at Ife.

"Bitch, what? Who the fuck you calling a whore? You don't know me for real for real." Ife shot back. She rolled her neck and her purple sisterlocs shifted off her shoulders.

"I don't need to see you on the corner passing out pussy to know that it goes down. I can spot a trick with one eye." Brisa explained as she matched Ife with a neck roll of her own that swung her long bob around her shoulders.

"And that's just what you gonna be left with if you keep coming for me, purrrrrr." Ife clapped back.

"Aight, aight hold up." Native said, making a late attempt to diffuse the situation she hoped would stop on its own.

"Ain't no hold up!" Ife continued. "I-."

"Cut the read off!" Native interrupted. "Brisa, this is Ife an old friend of mine. Ife, this is Brisa, a new friend of mine." Native explained finally making introductions.

Why the fuck would Native say that? Brisa was on fire.

"New friend?" She asked, staring daggers into Native's eyes. "Really, Native?"

Ife chuckled. "No wonder you doing the most. Yo ass new." She crossed her arms over her chest.

"Keep sniggling, bitch. I bet you'd find it very hard to laugh with all your teeth on this floor!" Brisa stated as she offered Ife up.

"Darling, I would end you and the gag is I wouldn't even break a sweat. Stamp." Ife shot back.

"Come on, man, this ain't the Real House Dykes of DC! Quit with all this drama. Bamma's starting to stare and shit." Native yelled.

"All I was doing was saying hi," Ife continued, having exposed the cracks of their relationship.

"It was good seeing you, Ife. But–."

"So it was good seeing her too?" Brisa said. "After all that shit?"

The thing was Native was done. So she grabbed Brisa's elbow and said, "Let's go, Bri."

"Don't Bri me, Native!" Brisa screamed giving zero fucks about who was staring at the scene. "You really done fucked up now." She yelled as she stormed off in rage.

Leaving Native standing there looking stupid.

Before Native moved, she looked back at Ife who mouthed, "Call me," winked and licked her lips before walking away.

Native shook her head.

Just that quick, all the work Native put into keeping Brisa appeased was gone.

Fuck.

# CHAPTER THREE
# BABY DOM

Baby Dom walked down the long hallway slowly as if approaching the electric chair. She had no idea what to expect.

The best thing about being in prison in her mind was the fact that one of her best friends, Mystro, would be there doing time with her. So to her, it was something like a party.

"Dent," the female C.O. called out to Baby Dom.

"Ye-yes ma'am," she replied faintly as she stepped up towards the window.

"Hold out your arms." The C.O. instructed.

Hesitantly Baby Dom complied with the command and held out her arms.

The corrections officer stuffed a pile into her grasp that contained a bed roll no thicker than three sheets, a blanket and a roll of toilet paper. Baby Dom almost fell over at the force.

"Follow me," another corrections officer told Baby Dom as she tried to situate the items in her arm before they hit the ground.

When she gained control, she quick stepped to where the C.O. was and fell back in line.

When he stopped walking, they were in front of a row of cells.

"You're in twenty-one down in the middle." He scanned the cells and advised.

Baby Dom stood motionless and eye-balled the officer.

"What? This part of the tour's over, go to your cell." He instructed.

"Oh, uh, which way is the kitchen?" She yawned and scratched her head. "I'm looking for a friend of mine."

"Friend?"

"Yeah, I know her from the–."

"This ain't no dorm! Put your stuff down first, inmate, then you can roam the tier." C.O. Michael advised before shaking his head and walking away.

It was as if Baby Dom had to will her legs to move before she could start to walk.

She was extremely frightened.

She knew she was in prison, but she thought she would have a little more guidance.

She was wrong.

After what seemed like forever, when she found her way in front of cell number twenty-one, C.O. Michael yelled down to the security desk, "Pop two one."

There was a loud buzz and then the cell door opened up slowly.

Baby Dom jumped back to let the steel gray automatic door with a small window fully open in front of her.

She took one last look at C.O. Michael who motioned for her to walk inside.

She did.

Slowly.

As if approaching her deathbed, she went deeper. Once completely inside, she was shocked and appalled at the condition of the small cell. She didn't know what she had in mind, but it definitely wasn't a garbage can.

No one was inside, but it was clear someone nasty lived there.

There was what looked like urine and toilet paper in the metal toilet that had a pungent odor like ammonia stemming from it.

Toothpaste was strewn all around the metal sink along with hair that was so bad it looked like it was growing out of the drain.

There were also magazines, underwear, and empty potato chip bags all over the floor.

It was completely disgusting.

"Damn," Baby Dom said to herself. "They coulda at least cleaned this bitch up."

She stepped over what she could on the floor and made her way to the bunk beds.

Even though she wanted to take her shit up out of there, she began to toss stuff off the bottom bunk onto the floor and laid her bed roll down. Afterall, it would be her home for a while.

"Aye, get that shit off my bunk, slim. That ain't your bed." A voice yelled out from behind her.

Baby Dom jumped up and turned around quickly to see who it was.

Before her stood her cellmate whose nickname was Bruiser.

She was tall, six feet to be exact, thin with brown skin and a faded haircut. If it wasn't for her A cup breasts you could easily mistake her for a man.

Baby Dom swallowed the lump in her throat before she spoke. "My bad fam, I really couldn't tell which bed was mine. Both bunks had a lot of shit on them." Baby Dom explained.

"The fuck you just say?" Bruiser asked.

What part didn't she understand? "I said they had a lot of shit on them so–."

"You going or something?"

Baby Dom, naive to most of the world, could sense in the stranger's tone that she said the wrong thing.

Maybe she could word it differently.

"I said I couldn't tell which one was mine 'cuz both of 'em was fucked up. I-I ain't mean no disrespect I just really couldn't tell." Baby Dom stated nervously.

"Oh, so you an 'ole sarcastic half dyke huh?" Bruiser asked, stepping closer.

She scratched her scalp. "Nah, fam I really wasn't trying to–"

"Yeah yeah yeah just watch yourself. 'Cuz if you really wasn't sure, you would've waited to ask questions before moving inside. And I don't give a fuck if you had to wait all night." Bruiser advised.

"Okay, you got it." Baby Dom looked around and gazed at both bunks, "so which one is mine again?"

"Do it look like I'm gonna be climbing up and down to get in and out of the bed to you?" Bruiser asked.

Baby Dom gave a look of confusion. Was she serious? "So...which...one...is...mine?"

"Man, get your ass on top!" Bruiser yelled out of frustration.

Baby Dom nodded her head and grabbed her things off the bottom bunk.

"Why the fuck your young ass in here anyway, shouldn't you be in juvie or something?" Bruiser asked.

"Nah, I know I'm jive short and little but I'm old enough to be here...they say I dropped a nigga."

"*They said,* huh?"

She nodded. "Yep. So I took a plea and gotta do a dime."

Baby Dom climbed up on the side of the bunk and began to toss Bruiser's stuff off the top bed.

"Aye, aye, aye...what the fuck is you doing now?" Bruiser yelled as her belongings hit the ground.

"What I do now, fam?" Baby Dom asked bewildered.

"You 'bout to get dropped! The fuck is you tossing my shit for?"

Baby Dom looked around at all the stuff already all over the place, shocked. She wasn't a hundred percent certain, but she had a feeling that her body was the freshest thing in that cell.

"So, what you want me to–."

"Just hand me my stuff, little nigga." Bruiser glared.

"My bad, here you go." Baby Dom removed the remaining clothes from the top bunk and gently passed them to her cellmate.

"What you slow or something?" Bruiser asked sincerely.

"Nah, not that I know of." Baby Dom answered seriously.

"Well, let me set you straight on how I run this shit here." Bruiser threw down the items she grabbed onto her bed and began to explain.

64

Baby Dom listened attentively.

"This is my cell." She pointed at the trashy floor. "In other words, this my house and you just a guest. Top bunk belongs to you. Everything that you can put on your top bunk and around your top bunk belongs to you, unless I want it for myself. Everywhere else in this house is my territory. If you gotta shit, you gotta ask to use my toilet."

Baby Dom looked confused. "Why I gotta do all that though?"

Bruiser shook her head. "I can see we not gonna get along too good."

Baby Dom lowered her gaze. "My bad."

Bruiser looked up at Baby Dom. "Where you from?"

"DC, Northeast." Baby Dom said proudly. "You know, Mystro? That's my homie, she in here too."

Bruiser knew exactly who she was asking about but didn't wanna let on that she knew.

"What the fuck is a Mystro?" Bruiser asked sarcastically. "She a fake ass conductor or something?"

"Conductor?"

"You know what...you dumb as fuck. Who you talking about though?"

"That's my folks name. Mystro. She cook in the kitchen." Baby Dom boasted as she made up her bunk.

"Never heard of her."

"That's cool. I'll introduce y'all when I find her. Can you tell me where the kitchen is?" Baby Dom asked excitedly.

"Do I look like your prison tour guide?"

"Not really."

"I can tell already, you in for a rough ride in here." Bruiser shook her head. "Go find the kitchen yourself!"

Native sat in the visitor's hall awaiting the inmates to be brought inside.

She sat at the brown table that was full of snacks which included bags of chips, candy, and grape sodas. While she waited, she observed the rest of the visitors.

There were men who were alone and some people with kids. Whole families that consisted of inmate's mother's, father's, children, siblings, and other people Native couldn't put her finger on.

But out of all the people to watch, no one was more fun than the single women there to visit their friends and girlfriends.

Some of the women were older and Native imagined them to be there to visit their girlfriend that may be doing serious time. Native started to wonder if she were in that predicament, would she stick around and do time with her shawty.

Probably not.

Native looked at the door the inmates normally came out of.

It remained closed.

She scanned the room again and noticed a girl who seemed to look through Native. The girl stared so hard Native had to turn around to check if someone was behind her.

There wasn't.

Shawty was doing the absolute most.

Native made a mental note to find out if Mystro had the intel on her.

Just as Native turned back around out of embarrassment, the door opened, and inmates filed into the visitor's hall.

Mystro walked in and sauntered over to Native. The two gave each other dap and embraced into a one-armed hug.

"Sooonnn...you don't know how good it is to see your ugly ass." Native stated.

"Fuck you, young! What's good?" Mystro shot back.

"Ain't shit for real. You ain't missing nothing out there," she lied.

Mystro nodded. "Well, good looking out on these vitals. I barely eat up in there, slim. Even with me sising the food as best I can, shit still tastes like shit to me, ya know?"

"Stamp!" Native laughed. "So, outside the food being fucked up...you good?"

Of course, she wasn't.

She was in prison.

"Good as I can be. I keep my head down, don't mix into too much and stay out the way." Mystro explained while she popped the top of her grape soda can. "But I know how I am, ain't a whole lot to tell in my life. What's going on out there though? Talk to me."

"So you gonna pretend everything–."

"I don't wanna discuss shit up in here right now." She said firmer. "So talk."

Native nodded. "Slim, Brisa is lunching!" She placed her hands on both sides of her head.

"You surprised?"

"I mean, I knew it might be tough when I decided to move in with shawty. You know how I like my freedom and all. But damn! I never expected this shit." Native vented.

Mystro laughed. "Don't fake."

"What you talking 'bout?"

"What you doing that got her fucked up with you?" Mystro asked while picking up a hot chicken wing that Native microwaved and blew on it. "Which side bitch you back on? Because I know you did something."

"My nigga, I ain't doing shit! I come home straight after work, for the most part anyway." Native explained.

"What that mean?" Mystro licked the buffalo sauce off her fingers.

"I'm saying, I might stop off at the bar every now and again to get a drink before I go home. Not every day though."

"Why? You ain't got bottles at your crib?" Mystro asked while digging into a bag of salt and vinegar potato chips.

70

She was snacking like she never ate before.

"Dog, after being up in that call center all day arguing with motherfuckas on the phone, I don't feel like coming home and arguing with shawty. And lately, that's all it's been. Crazy ass arguing. I feel like anything I do ain't good enough for her, man. Shit wearing on me." Native confessed.

"I feel you." She wiped her mouth and leaned back in her seat.

"So yeah, every now and again I grab a drink first to calm my nerves. If that's a problem, it's whatever."

Mystro looked at Native with a smirk.

"What now?" Native leaned closer.

"Look, you signed on the dotted line with Brisa. That means you can't just up and cut out on her."

"Hold up, I ain't marry that lady!" Native yelled.

Mystro cut her eyes towards the C.O. who shot her table a vicious look after Native's outburst.

She put her hands out palms down to let him know everything was cool.

"Slim, relax for you get us tossed out of here." Mystro whispered.

Native balled her fist up to her mouth to quiet down. "My bad."

"I'm just saying, you made a commitment."

"Whatever."

"And I ain't say you married her, I'm talking about signing the lease and moving in with her. That means you responsible for rent being paid. You can't just dip 'cuz she get on your nerves." Mystro schooled.

"I never said I was dipping on her, moe. Just need to get right sometimes before I go home and deal with the bullshit." Native explained. She wiped her hands down her gray sweatpants.

"But what you think that means to her? Maybe she feel like you not coming home because you not feeling her."

Native thought Mystro was on some relationship therapy shit but she would leave it alone.

"This why a nigga prefers the single life."

Mystro shook her head. "Brisa tight with you all the time 'cuz you being selfish. Try telling her where you coming from. You ever think 'bout that?" Mystro asked.

"I did, but I ain't feel like arguing with her because of it either. She knew I was a pussy hound before we got together. She'll fuck around and think I'm resorting back to my old ways." Native admitted.

"You don't know that. You can't act on what you think she might do. You a grown ass dyke, son. Tell that lady that she pressing you and you need a little space every now and again but that don't mean you cheating. She insecure 'cuz that's exactly how you make her feel."

Native sat in silence biting her bottom lip.

"Being in a relationship is give and take son. You give and they take." Mystro joked. "Sometimes you could land in bad patches, but if you don't talk about how you feeling with her, you may never get to how good it can be, dig?" Mystro stated.

Native looked up at her. She inhaled deeply before letting out a big breath.

"You right, fuck, I ain't got shit to lose. I mean, we beefing now all the time anyway, might as well get this shit off my chest."

"There you go." Mystro smiled. She put her soda can down. "And if the shit don't work, at least you can say you tried and have a clear conscience and peace of mind. Your peace has to be paramount." Mystro continued.

"Paramount, huh?" Native nodded and smiled. "Speaking of clearing your conscience...Breezy reached out to me."

Mystro shifted in her seat.

74

"Can you go get me some more wings before they all gone?" Mystro asked Native, avoiding the statement.

Native shot Mystro a knowing look.

"Skipping the subject huh?"

Mystro sucked her teeth and wiped her nose with the back of her hand. "You gonna get them or what?"

Native looked at her once more before she grabbed the zip lock bag full of quarters that sat on their table and walked up to the vending machine. She put in the correct amount of change needed and pushed the button to select the buffalo wings.

Once done, she walked them over to the microwave and put them in before looking back at Mystro.

Inmates weren't allowed to leave their seats once they were at the table. So Native was playing waiter. If they had to use the restroom, the C.O.'s would call out and ask and any inmate that had to pee needed to line up.

Prison was on that kindergarten type treatment.

When the wings were zapped completely, Native put the hot bag on paper towels and took them back to the table.

Mystro immediately dug into them.

"Slim, fucking up that chicken ain't gonna get you out of responding to what I said." Native reminded her. "As a matter of fact, every time I move the convo to you, you eating and shit."

"What you talking 'bout?" Mystro asked while blowing on a wing to cool it down.

"I just said it." Native frowned. "Let's talk Breezy." She clapped once. "Why you carrying her?" Native inquired.

Before Mystro answered, she put her chicken wing down, wiped her hands and mouth on a hard brown paper towel and looked at Native.

"Son, don't come at me 'bout no Breezy!"

"What you saying, you can kick all that fatherly advice to me about my lil' situation

76

BY C. WASH

but I can't shed no light on yours? How fucked up is that?" Native asked.

Mystro looked away. "I was just trying to help."

"My bad, My. I ain't mean it like that." Native explained. "I'm just saying...bammas be real ready to kick knowledge to another motherfucka going through it, but never take they own words as truth."

Mystro wiped her hand down her face and thought about her daddy who died not too long ago. She knew Native didn't mean any harm but still hated the reminder that her pops was gone.

She took a deep breath before she addressed her friend.

"I'm just not about to jump all into another chick, Nae. I mean doing that got me in this bitch in the first place. I ain't signing up for that shit again." Mystro explained as she straightened out her white prison issued scrub top.

"I can dig it...But just know, one thing ain't got shit to do with the other. They two different women, My. Church was a scandalous hoe. Square biz! You know it and I know it too." Native protested. "But Breezy different. You know that too deep down. Don't make her suffer behind the bullshit you went through with Church."

"But even if I take heed to your words of wisdom, I could be in here for ten years, Native. Ten." She threw up both hands. "I ain't trying to put slim through that, man. Or worse...Say I stop being cold to her and we get tight, then two or three years down the road she stops coming. Then I'm up in this bitch heartbroken looking dumb as shit. Nah, fuck that." She looked down and shook her head.

Native stared at Mystro before speaking. "Or what if she the one, and she do every damn day of this time with you? Plus, nigga you won't be doing the whole ten no way. I gotta rack say you coming out in three if not before.

You still in the law library working on your appeal, right?"

Mystro picked up another chicken wing and bit into it. "Man, let's change the subject," she said, "Baby Dom arrived on the block. You knew she was coming here?" Mystro asked.

Baby Dom coming in there was the one thing that rattled Mystro's mind ever since she saw her earlier. She didn't want it for her...the prison life and she tried to control that. But it was no longer her call.

"Yeah, she told me." Native stated.

"I hate seeing her in here! I was gonna do the time for her, Native. I was gonna take this shit on because I know she not built like that. It's like...it's like..."

"Your little brother is in jail with you," Native said, completing her sentence.

"Yeah, and if niggas find out we close, they gonna use it against her."

"Look, I know you mad at her but she still fam, slim. You gotta look out for--"

"I ain't gotta do shit but my time!" Mystro barked grabbing the attention of two C.O.'s. "Nothing more, nothing less. So don't put that on me."

She looked at them and fixed her greasy fingers into praying motion to plead for forgiveness, letting them know she would stay in check.

"One more outburst from your table and your visit's over inmate." C.O. Smith yelled.

Mystro nodded in defeat and agreement.

"Let's not talk no more 'bout all this emotional shit before they cut our visit short." Native stated. "Because it's obvious neither one of us can handle it right now."

"No bull." Mystro laughed.

"Say," Native began, "Who shawty with the bad wig over by the door?"

Mystro looked up from the table and quickly scanned the large room until her eyes settled on the main door. She assessed the woman and the inmate sitting with her.

"I don't know the broad but she with Bruiser." Mystro said referring to Baby Dom's cellmate.

"Well, she was eye fucking the hell outta me when I got in here," Native proclaimed. "Before y'all walked inside. Look, she staring now."

Mystro focused back on the inmate and her guest.

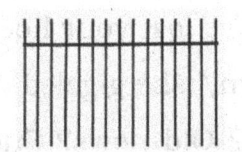

## ACROSS THE ROOM

"What the fuck are you looking at?" Bruiser asked her lady. The dimples in her cheeks on full display even though she was annoyed.

Girlfriend cut her eyes between Mystro, Native and Bruiser.

"I could swear them two used to do shows down the Delta. They didn't do it long before they started doing privates."

"Shows?" Bruiser shrugged. "That's what you call it when Doms slither around the stage lip syncing to another nigga's song?"

Her girlfriend ignored her question. "I'm mad I never got a chance to get a show. They had all the bitches keyed up!" She licked her lips.

Bruiser couldn't believe the level of disrespect broadcast in her face.

"You must've lost your hoetic ass mind!"

"Calm down," she giggled. "It's old news."

"Old news? Old news? Fuck is you telling me for then?"

"Would you fucking relax!"

"Bitch!" Bruiser jumped up, smacked the shit out of her girlfriend and stared down at her. "Play with me again. Next time I'm knocking out your teeth!"

She remained on her feet less than fifteen seconds before C.O. Smith rushed toward the scene, grabbed Bruiser and threw her to the ground where she was cuffed.

An alarm began blaring loudly.

"Visitation is now over! Inmates line up!"

# CHAPTER FOUR
# NATIVE

After speaking to Mystro, Native felt that maybe she could do better. At least she would try.

"Baby, can we talk? You've been ignoring me the whole day now." Native pleaded. "Let's cut out all this weak ass shit."

She reached to grab Brisa's tiny, manicured hand but Brisa just side-eyed her.

"Talk about what, Native? How you disrespected me? How you made me look like a whole fool in the middle of the mall in front of your little girlfriend? Is that what you want to talk about?" Brisa asked.

"She not my girlfriend and you know that. I can't control who shop and where they shop."

"I knew you was out here twirling, that just proves my point."

"Twirling?" Native could do without such a soft ass tag.

"I'm so sick of feeling like this." Brisa said with a look of defeat in her eyes.

"Like what?"

"That you cheating on me!" Brisa yelled.

"Man, I told you I'm not cheating, what more do I gotta do?" Native asked with her shoulders raised and palms toward the ceiling.

"Then who was that bitch?" Brisa asked, crossing her arms over her breasts.

"Just a friend from my past. I haven't seen her in almost a year. We had an entire conversation about this already. It's like you reuse old fights for later. Do you even listen to me?"

"Oh no, honey she is way more than just a friend the way she was talking. I'm not an idiot." She placed her hands on her hips.

Native paused.

"Tell me I'm lying." Brisa stared up at Native for validation. "You can't." She pointed a red manicured nail in her face.

"Look, man I really don't know what you want me to say. Shawty and me just friends. We was cool as shit and that's it. And again, I ain't talked to her or seen her in-"

"Did you fuck her?" Brisa asked, tilting her head to the side with raised eyebrows.

Native swallowed the lump in her throat.

She had to carefully weigh her answer.

She took a deep breath and was about to confess that her and Ife had messed around sexually in the past when her cell phone rang.

Literally saved by the bell.

"Who's calling you right now!" Brisa screamed.

Native did a sigh of relief as she turned to grab her phone off the table. When she saw the number, she immediately took the call.

"Yeah, I'll accept. Aye...what's up, fam? You good?" Native asked. She bowed her head to await Mystro's reply.

"What's up, homie, yeah I'm cool. Busy?"

"Native!" Brisa called her name while she shot daggers in her direction. "You gonna do me like this?"

"Uh, nah, I'm not busy I can talk what's up?" Native put her index finger up in Brisa's direction.

Their conversation was useless anyway.

"So, you not busy? You know what...fuck you, Native." Brisa yelled as she stormed off into the bedroom and slammed the door.

"Aye, slim if you can't talk it's cool, I'll just call you tomorrow." Mystro said as she heard Brisa yelling through the phone.

"Hell no, I'm good. You just saved my whole life for real for real. I ain't get a chance to tell you I ran into Ife while shopping with Brisa at the mall." Native stated while making sure Brisa wasn't near.

"What? Awww nah! How the fuck you forget to tell me that shit!" Mystro asked.

"Man, I tried to avoid her when I seen her but you know Ife, once she spotted me she was having none of it. So she approached us and you know Brisa, she already suspects I'm out here being the biggest freak."

"Ife always on some other shit."

"Tell me about it. Next thing I know you would have thought they was on RuPaul's Drag Race 'cuz they got to reading each other right there in the middle of the mall." Native explained. She looked toward the direction of the bedroom.

No Brisa.

Mystro busted out laughing.

"Slim, this shit not hardly funny that lady is in the other room right now on fire. I ain't used to all this, man. I don't know what to do."

"My bad I don't mean to laugh I just know what it was probably giving right there in the middle of the spot. How the hell did you get out of there without them fighting anyway?"

"Barely that's how, barely. And now I'm in here dealing with this aftermath. I'm scared to go to sleep tonight and the worst thing about

BY C. WASH

it all is I ain't even fucking shawty. Tell me what to do, bro."

"First thing you need to do is be honest with Brisa."

"Man, hell no!" Native yelled out before realizing how loud she was being and lowered her voice. "If she knew how me and Ife wild fucked off and on, she will pack my shit and toss me out." She whispered.

"First off, she can't kick you out of your own spot. Second, she can smell that fake shit from a mile away."

"Just thinking about it makes me want to give it a hard no." Native placed her hand on her forehead.

"If I know you, you dodging her questions. Be straight up with her."

"Being straight up...What do that look like to you son?" Native asked seriously.

"Man, I don't know, tell her shawty wanted more with you than you were willing to give at the time. And now seeing you walking in the mall with your girlfriend probably made her jealous so she acted a ass." Mystro explained.

"I don't know..."

"I mean you can't guess what the woman was trying to do but I'm willing to bet that Brisa will understand that explanation." She continued. "It's called growth, champ. You've done a lot of it with her, so show her that."

Native was quiet as she took everything in.

"You still there, nigga? You know my time on here short." Mystro asked.

"Yeah, man I'm still here. That makes sense actually. I just hope she's trying to hear me."

"She'll hear you, trust me show your soft dom side." Mystro chuckled.

Native sucked her teeth. "Here you go. Aight, so what's good? You seen Baby Dom yet?" Native asked.

"Nah, I told you, I ain't trying to be connected with slim." Mystro answered.

"Look, now I realize you pissed at the youngin' for what she did in court," Native got serious. "But facts is facts, she in there 'cuz she was looking out for you. Remember that."

Mystro sighed. "Whatever, man."

"You need to find her and get square with her to watch her back. Period."

# Chapter Five
## MYSTRO

**M**ystro was in her cell reading her favorite T. Styles novel, *"War"*.

She had a few minutes down time before she had to head to the kitchen.

She had her face deep in her book when she felt someone staring at her.

"So you ain't got no love for me no more, fam?" Baby Dom said to Mystro in the hallway in front of Mystro's cell.

Mystro looked up from her reading and sighed.

Baby Dom still looked the same, except instead of basketball shorts and Jay's on her feet, she donned a white prison issued uniform and black slides.

Her shoulder length locs neat and pulled back with a simple hair tie.

"Baby Dom, why you here?" Mystro closed her book, sat up and asked with a look of disappointment on her face.

"I gotta do the dime on that nut ass nigga I dropped. I thought you –"

"Naw, champ...why you standing in front of my house?" Mystro, now on her feet, stood motionless while she stared Baby Dom down with disgust.

"You calling this your house?"

"What you want?"

Baby Dom cleared her throat. "I came looking for you. I know you be in the kitchen but when I slid by there I ain't see you. I like the temple taper, fam. Shit look torch! When you decide to cut out the rows...when you got in here? Needed a change or ain't nobody in here that can keep you tightened up?" Baby Dom rambled, one question and statement after the other.

Mystro took a deep breath before she addressed her.

"You talk too much. If you hadn't popped off at the mouth, you wouldn't even be in here." She rolled her eyes. "You not supposed to be in here."

"But I couldn't sit there and let you take the whole beef. I took the nigga out and I gotta pay for it. It's cool, fam 'cuz at least we here with each other. Now we here for each other too." Baby Dom explained.

Mystro stood in her silence boiling with rage.

Before she replied to Baby Dom, she took a deep breath then grabbed her ID card off her bunk.

"You did the exact opposite of what I wanted you to do."

"But–."

"Ain't no but. You wanted to be in here, well be in here alone."

"What that...what that mean?"

"I'm not here for you...Stay the fuck away from me." Mystro advised before she walked

94

past her and out of her cell leaving Baby Dom to sort it out on her own.

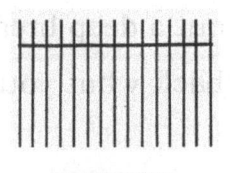

## BRUISER

"Aye, how come this my third time calling you today? Where the fuck you been?" Bruiser yelled into the phone receiver at her girlfriend.

She was at the end of the phone bank hallway using the last phone on the wall.

Her weak attempt at privacy. Everybody was still in the business.

"Hello... Hello?" Bruiser repeated.

"Yeah." Her girlfriend dryly replied.

"What the fuck you doing? Did you hear me?" Bruiser raised her eyebrows and asked intensely.

"Hold on." Girlfriend said.

"I'm going to fucking snap her neck." Bruiser whispered to herself. "Hello!"

"Yeah, I said hold on." She repeated.

Bruiser let out a deep breath.

"Yeah, I'm back what you say?" Girlfriend asked.

"You know where I am right?" Bruiser asked her as she gripped the phone receiver so hard it almost snapped in her hand.

"Um, yeah." Girlfriend rolled her eyes. "What that mean?"

"So you know I can't lay hands on you but the last time you was in my presence you felt me." Bruiser reminded her. "Didn't you?"

"Mmm hmmm."

"When I call you, stop everything and take that shit. No excuses." Bruiser demanded.

"Aye, Bruiser, let me use five minutes on your phone code right quick!" Another inmate walked up on Bruiser and asked.

"Nigga, don't you see I'm on a motherfucking call? Get out my face."

"Who are you talking to?" Bruiser's girlfriend said into the phone.

"Oh, so now you can hear everything that's said?" She asked, redirecting her attention.

"Constance, I don't feel like being on the phone and have to deal with you yelling at me. I already feel some kind of way about what happened on the visit." Her girlfriend admitted. "You put your hands on me."

"Don't act like I ain't do it before."

"In public!"

Bruiser sighed.

"Look, I was calling you to apologize for that. I don't know what got in me. But for real, you was dead wrong sizing up them bammas right in my face." Bruiser defended.

"I didn't mean nothing by it. I was shocked when I saw them sitting in there. I mean I had heard one of them killed their manager chick, but I ain't know how true it was. My bad, Constance." Girlfriend apologized.

"My bad too. I shouldn't have snapped." Bruiser admitted. "Got a new cellmate that's annoying AF and it turns out she may know them bitches you was gawking all over, so I really just blew up. You know I ain't mean it, girl."

"So, you and Mystro cellmates now?" She said excitedly. "Oh my God, that's so cool. What kind of person is she?" Bruiser's girlfriend didn't hear a word she said.

"Young, are you high or something? I said I got a new cellmate that knows 'em, not that she's my cellmate now. Besides that fact, why the fuck are you still asking me about that bitch?" Bruiser asked as her nostrils flared.

Bruiser's girlfriend was quiet.

"You mad or something?"

"I don't give a fuck about no Mystro. It's bad enough her little funky ass friend is in my cell, now I gotta keep hearing you talk about this bitch too? Don't make me come through this phone!" Bruiser yelled.

"I'm sorry, Constance."

**BY C. WASH**

Bruiser snapped. "Stop calling me that! It's Con or Bruiser you know that."

"Ok, Connnnnnn." She over exaggerated the nickname.

"Con, come on man, I gotta check in with my folks right quick." The inmate interrupted. "Let me use you-"

"If I tell you one more time...I'ma smack the shit out you." Bruiser said to the annoying inmate through clenched teeth.

The inmate moved away so quickly, it was as if she vanished into the walls.

"When you gonna put that money on my books? I gotta get store next week." Bruiser said to her girlfriend.

Silence.

"Hello?" Bruiser yelled into the receiver.

"Oh, you talking to me now?" Her girlfriend asked facetiously.

"Is everybody around me stuck on stupid? The fuck!" Bruiser looked back and yelled.

"Pipe down, Patterson!" C.O. Michael said as he walked up to the phone bank.

Bruiser gritted her teeth and turned back around.

"The money," Bruiser said on the phone through clenched teeth. "When are you gonna do it?"

"Oh, yeah I'll do it tomorrow." Her girlfriend replied.

With that out the way, it was time to get down to some other shit. So Bruiser looked around, bent her head lower in an attempt to shield her conversation.

"What you got on?" Her mouth was so close to the handset it was as if she were tongue kissing it.

"Huh?"

"I said, what you wearing?" Bruiser asked again.

"Oh, my onesie and my bonnet."

Bruiser stood up straight.

Blown.

**BY C. WASH**

"Come on, man, even if that's really what you got on you supposed to tell me some sexy shit. You know I need to hear that! The fuck kind of fantasy I'm supposed to--"

"Pssst...Bruiser, can I use five minutes on your card," another inmate asked. "I promise you won't--"

"You know what, if one more nigga get on my neck I'm going off! When I'm done if it's time left, you can pay for it. But don't be pressing me about no–."

"Aight...aight all this time you yelling, you wasting minutes." The annoying inmate snapped back. "I already gave you the noodles. You said you–."

"Cuz you keep bothering me when–."

*The call has ended.* The phone's automatic system stated before the call was disconnected.

"Fuck!" Bruiser yelled out.

Now she wanted somebody to pay.

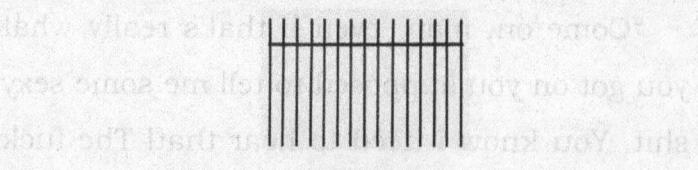

# MYSTRO

Mystro was in the kitchen prepping for tomorrow's meal. As she checked the pantry, C.O. Michael walked inside.

Mystro noticed him and immediately walked out and over to the oven, opened it and released the overpowering fragrance of food cooking.

C.O. Michael pulled up a stool and plopped on it while he waited in anticipation of his feast.

He watched closely as Mystro went about her business.

In automatic mode, Mystro put on an oven mitt and pulled out a tray that warmed her special taste test meal of meatloaf, mashed potatoes, and cornbread.

C.O. Michael jumped up excitedly and walked over to the sink to wash his hands as

**BY C. WASH**

Mystro transferred the food onto a plate and placed it on the table.

"Nowwww we gonna see how good you really are." C.O. Michael said rubbing his hands together in anticipation of eating a version of his favorite meal.

"Can't wait to hear what you think." Mystro admitted. "But keep in mind, I don't have all my ingredients."

"Aye, look. No matter how it tastes, thank you, Mystro. You have no idea. I been dreaming of this all day." C.O. Michael confessed as he smiled brightly and pulled the stool up to the table ready to devour his plate.

Mystro nodded her head and awaited his reaction.

C.O. Michael picked up his spork and cut into the meatloaf as Mystro watched him place the food in his mouth.

She looked for any sign of approval.

C.O. Michael didn't disappoint. He closed his eyes while he chewed to savor the taste then smiled. "Mmmmm...better than my mama's." He laughed. "She was the only one who could make this for me."

"Go head, young." Mystro said, removing the oven mitt from her hand.

"I'm serious."

"How it's gonna be better than your mama's? Look at where we are?"

"You gotta learn to take a compliment." He repositioned the keys that dangled on his utility belt to give his belly room to expand.

Mystro shook her head and laughed. "Well, I'm happy to oblige."

"Listen," C.O. Michael started while he swallowed the food he was chewing. "I know I'm new around here and I'm a C.O., but I been here long enough to know what's happening." He wiped his mouth with a hard brown paper towel that resembled a paper bag.

"What you mean?" Mystro asked.

"I was just up near the phone bank and overheard Bruiser going off on her girlfriend about you." He took another bite. "Mentioned

104

her celly, your folks, and how she knows you too."

Mystro was stunned.

She had no idea that Bruiser and Baby Dom were cellmates. Much less, that Baby Dom must have been talking about her.

"What folks?" Mystro questioned fishing to see what he knew. She really tried to keep her personal business to herself but it wasn't working.

"New inmate. The 'lil jawn that bunks with Patterson." C.O. Michael continued in his strong Philly accent. "Stop playing."

Mystro was on fire.

Her nostrils flared.

She turned away from C.O. Michael to calm down.

"I don't know why, but Patterson's got it in for you Mystro...Majorly. She found out you and her celly was cool outside of here and may use that some kind of way later to get at you."

"But I ain't did shit to slim. I'm just doing my time and cooking. Fuck she got it in for me for?" Mystro questioned.

"I'm told that ever since you got here, her stock went down. Not to mention that little scuffle she got into with her girlfriend in the visitor's hall." He explained. "You remember? You was on a visit in the hall too."

Mystro knew exactly what he was talking about. How could she not? That little stunt shut visitation down for a month.

"I was there but what that got to do with me?"

"The fight was because she was looking in you and your friend's direction." He paused. "So she had to do time in isolation behind that. And if you ask me, she blames you." He said with his mouth open wide chewing potatoes.

"Nah, man. We was minding our business when her girl started staring at us?" Mystro explained.

"Look, the girl sees it differently. And other females have been checking you out too. She

**106**

used to be king in here, but as of late, it hasn't been that." C.O. Michael stated.

"No offense, but again, what do that gotta do with me? My homie told me shawty was eyeballing her while they were waiting before I even came out. So, how I get charged with that beef?" Mystro asked with her hands raised.

"I don't know, but I'm guessing that was the final straw for Patterson. I think you just need to make sure you keep your friend close. Bruiser may not be able to rattle you, but she may try to make her life miserable."

Mystro was beyond pissed.

During her short stint there, she quickly learned how the prison rules went.

She knew that Bruiser could make trouble for her and get in the way of her getting out of there early.

She had to figure out how to end this shit before it even kicked off.

# CHAPTER SIX
## MYSTRO

**M**ystro had her head deep in a book in the law library.

She had a lawyer that was actively working on her appeal and although she was no lawyer, she vowed to try and assist him in any way possible.

While she reviewed case law similar to her situation, out of the corner of her eye she saw Bruiser walk into the library alone.

This was different because outside of visitation, Bruiser always had at least one flunky with her.

"You ever tried the crab cake egg roll at Eddie's?" Bruiser strolled up to Mystro and asked.

Mystro kept her head down but raised her eyes up to look at Bruiser. "What you say?"

"I said have you ever tried the crab cake egg roll from Eddie's?" She repeated.

"Nah... I can't say that I have." Mystro answered and looked back down at her book.

"Yeah, they got the buffalo chicken and steak and cheese egg roll too. But that Maryland crab cake joint is they best one." Bruiser advised with a look of nostalgia in her eyes.

Mystro nodded and kept reading.

"You should try putting that shit on the menu here. I know it'll be torch." Bruiser recommended.

"It sounds like it would be a good idea, but I doubt I can do that. I don't get those type of ingredients." Mystro focused back on her case in an attempt to ignore Bruiser, hoping she would bounce, while at the same time, keeping her in her peripherals in case she didn't.

When she didn't move, Mystro looked back up.

"Was there anything else?" Mystro asked.

"Yeah, I know you from DC, but I really don't know from what part?" Bruiser asked.

"Northeast." Mystro replied flatly.

"Thought so." Bruiser nodded her head and smirked. She rubbed her hair from the middle of her head towards the front to smooth out her waves.

Mystro looked at her book again.

"You not gonna ask me what part I'm from?" Bruiser said thirsty.

"I mean...I gotta lot of reading to -"

"Southwest. Yeah, I used to be down *Zanzibar* tough, and stayed down *The Warf* you know? That's my stomping grounds. Shit, I been here so long I know home don't even look like home no more." Bruiser rambled as she looked off into the distance.

Mystro sighed.

"You know *Captain White's* not even down *The Wharf?* They rolled out after all these years." She stated as she pulled out the brown chair and sat down at the wooden table across from Mystro.

Mystro stared at her blankly. She wasn't in the mood for conversation.

BY C. WASH

"I can't even imagine being down there and not seeing that joint, young!" Bruiser continued. "I mean I wouldn't even know how to act, you feel me?"

Mystro raised her eyebrows.

She really just wanted this bamma out her face. The name and place dropping was getting a bit old.

"Oh, but don't get me wrong just 'cuz I'm from Southwest don't mean I ain't travel throughout the city." Bruiser continued. "I also stayed at *Tracks* in Southeast. Damn, that was my jump off spot. I met all kinda bitches there."

"Is there something else I can help you with?" Mystro asked. She couldn't take it anymore.

Bruiser glared.

"What's the matter, my breath stink or something? I got some shit on my face? I mean I came in here all nice or whatever trying to hold a conversation with you about where we

111

both from and you act like you ain't trying to be bothered."

Mystro returned her glare and didn't blink. Bruiser smiled.

"I don't want no static, I just really came in here to give you a snack. You like Twinkies?" She asked, pulling the plastic wrapped sponge cake from out of her scrubs.

Mystro rolled her eyes. Fuck was this about?

"Like I said I got a lot of work to do so miss me with all the twinkies, crab cake egg rolls and the stroll down the DC streets. Get to your real point of being over here or dip."

Bruiser laughed. "Aight, bet. Hear me and hear me good! Stay the fuck away from my bitch!" She said with a pointed finger in Mystro's direction. "Is that to the point enough for you?"

"Your bitch?" Mystro shrugged.

"Myyyyyy bitch." Bruiser repeated in a strong whisper.

"Champ, I don't even know shawty." Mystro rubbed her hand through her curls.

"Well, that ain't what she said. She can't stop talking about how you and your little friend was all up in the Delta passing out dances and shit like whores." Bruiser explained. "She seems to know you pretty well."

"Listen, you got it all fucked up. Yes, I used to dance in the gay club in DC a couple years ago, but I never met your girl personally." Mystro explained. So, if she was a fan, it's–."

"A fan?" Bruiser glared.

"I mean ain't that what we talking about? Somebody you feeling, who saw us at our shows, and were feeling us?" Mystro asked, looking for clarity.

Bruiser was enraged. Her girl was definitely giving fan, but she wouldn't tell her. "Look, just stay away from mine."

"Or what?" Mystro raised one eyebrow and glared directly into Bruiser's face.

"Or, I may just have to get extra acquainted with my new cellmate." Bruiser said as she winked and raised her six-foot frame out of the chair. "Don't you wish you took the Twinkie now?" She laughed and walked away.

BY C. WASH

# CHAPTER SEVEN
## MYSTRO

"**B**aby Dom! Didn't I tell you not to be speaking about us in this mothafucka!" Mystro stormed into Baby Dom and Bruiser's cell yelling.

She found Baby Dom alone.

"Hey fam! Did you see that I folded up your laundry for you? I left it on your bunk." Baby Dom replied, ignoring Mystro's angry inquiry. She was so happy to see her.

"Yeah! And I don't want you doing that shit either! Listen, you need to act like we don't even know each other in here. What part of that don't you get?" Mystro held her arms out and asked.

"I don't get none of it. Why would we act like we don't know each other? We fammo." Baby Dom said confused.

"BD, in here we not family! This is why I wished you just kept ya mouth shut in court. Before you got here all I had to worry about was doing my time and trying to get back home as soon as I could. Now I got niggas coming to me talking about you like we best friends -"

"But we are best friends though...Ain't we?" Baby Dom asked, squinting her eyes.

"No!!" Mystro screamed and then looked around to check her surroundings. "We nothing in here! We was that out there." She pointed over her head.

Baby Dom looked up at her with sad eyes.

"I cannot control that they put you in this facility where I am. But what I can control is that I gotta look out for me and only me. You gotta look out for you, since you chose to be big and bad and speak up for yourself with the judge, after I told you not to, keep that same energy." Mystro yelled. "In here, you do not know me. I ain't got time to worry about us both."

"But...can't I look out for me and still be cool with you?" Baby Dom pleaded.

Mystro rolled her eyes and put her hands on top of her head in anger.

When she scanned the cell she noticed a picture above the top bunk that was of her, Native and Baby Dom on the porch of Native's mother's house.

"The fuck?"

Baby Dom followed Mystro's eyes to her picture.

"Take that shit down! That's what the fuck I'm talking 'bout. You got that broad coming to try and check me on shit I ain't got nothing to do with. Now, I see why she at my neck." Mystro continued with the veins in her forehead popping.

"But I still don't understand why we can't be friends in here."

"Baby Dom, this is prison. Niggas will use all kinds of stuff to get under your skin. If you cool with somebody, they may try to use that against you to get what they want. There are a lot of things you have to learn about prison life, but you gonna have to learn it on your own. I can't be your guide."

"But wouldn't it make more sense if we stuck together? It gotta be better with two than just one." Baby Dom stated.

"I told you, I'm trying to leave this place! I don't have time for all that. You do you and stay away from me. Trust me, it's for your own good too. You got it?" Mystro asked with her palms facing the ceiling.

Baby Dom's shoulders dropped in defeat. "Ok." She said as tears welled up in her eyes.

# CHAPTER EIGHT
## MYSTRO

Mystro was pissed after her conversation with Baby Dom and needed to vent. She went straight to the phone bank and hoped she didn't have to wait in line to make a call.

She didn't. There was nobody on the phones which was unusual.

*"You have a collect call from..."* The automatic recording stated.

"Mystro."

*"An inmate at Washington Alley Prison for Women. Do you accept the charges?"*

"Yessss sirrrrr." Native yelled.

The call connected.

"What up, son you busy?" Mystro asked angrily.

"Nah, what's good, fam? I'm glad you hit me. You get a chance to connect with Baby Dom yet?" Native inquired.

"Man, that's exactly what I'm calling you about, this shit is fucked up. She in here running her mouth already." Mystro spewed.

"Aye, come on, son you know how BD act! That ain't nothing new, but what she do?"

"So, I gave her the rules. Told her to act like we ain't know each other and what do she go and do...Be hot as fuck and puts a picture up of us over her bunk. Now what the fuck I'm supposed to do 'bout that?" Mystro looked behind her to check her surroundings.

"Hold up, My. I don't think I understand, tell me what you really mad about." Native said wanting to make sure she heard her correctly.

"It's like this, I'm trying to get home. I've been doing good in here because I've been keeping my head down and keeping to myself. I'd probably not talk to nobody if I didn't have a job in the kitchen but that's the extent of what I do. I'm in the law library, the kitchen or my cell. Then, Baby Dom shows up, and you know I'm already tight that she's even doing

time in the first place. Now I gotta worry about-
-"

"Aye, aye...Hold up, slim, so am I hearing you right?" Native asked confused. "Basically you saying the same thing you done already said. It's like you gotta say it repeatedly to convince yourself you in the right."

"What you talking 'bout?" Mystro replied.

"Yeah, she should have kept quiet in court, but that's not the type of person she is. That girl may have a lot with her, but she's always been loyal."

Mystro sighed and looked up.

"And no matter how it went down, had she not pulled that trigger you may not be here at all. You forget that already?" Native reminded her. "Because I hadn't."

The truth was, if Baby Dom hadn't shot Grover Lawrence, Church's boyfriend, when she did, he may have killed Mystro.

"Man, nah, I ain't forget. It's just crazy in here and I was not trying to let it get to me, but with BD here now, niggas already starting to come at me sideways, Native." Mystro admitted.

"Listen, fam, I'm not even gonna begin to act like I know what you going through in there. But I know this, it gotta be a little better having family do that time with you. I know it is for Baby Dom. She needs you, Mystro, even if you feel like you don't need her."

Mystro was speechless.

This wasn't what she intended on getting when she picked up the phone to call her homie.

Although, she had to admit, she was absolutely right.

Mystro let out a deep breath.

"Man...I hear you." Mystro stated. She put her head down and gripped the back of her neck. "It just put a wrench in everything I had planned."

"Sometimes family does."

"I'ma have to find a way to deal with this shit so she's good and I stay out of trouble too."

"There's my nigga!" Native shouted.

Mystro chuckled.

"Eye of the tiger, champ. You know what's waiting on you when you get out. Family, love, foolery and fuckery like we used to do. Plus, all the pussy you can handle."

Mystro laughed harder. "Nigga, you know that's the last thing on my mind."

"Oh yeah, I'm sure you getting tossed cheeks left and right in there huh?" Native asked sarcastically.

"You crazy as hell, I'm not sliding into nothing in this bitch." Mystro raised one eyebrow and shot back.

The two friends continued to laugh.

As their laughter wound down, Mystro noticed Bruiser walking up to the phone banks.

"Oh lawd, here this bamma go." Mystro advised. She switched the phone receiver from her left into her right hand.

"What's up?" Native questioned.

123

"Dom lady, the one that got our visit shut down, coming this way." Mystro whispered.

"Man, fuck that dyke, son! What you got on?" Native asked jokingly.

Mystro snickered and turned her back in Bruiser's direction so she could answer Native with some privacy.

"My prison issued cocaine white scrubs and slides. Why, what you got on?" Mystro asked in a sexy playful tone.

"Some jeans, some Yeezy's and a button down." Native replied.

"Damn, that sound good to me right about now. I sooooo can't wait to get home and get into that shit." Mystro stated referring to wearing regular clothes again.

*"You have 1 minute remaining."* The recorded operator stated.

"Aight, that's my queue. I appreciate you talking me down and setting me straight." Mystro said.

"Always, fam. You got this! Love your ass, hit me on the email."

124

"Love you too! Aight, bet." Mystro finished before hanging up the receiver.

As she walked back to her cell, she had no idea that Bruiser overheard the last part of her conversation and glared in Mystro's direction, completely ready to snap.

# CHAPTER NINE
## MYSTRO
## A WEEK LATER

**M**ystro took a deep breath.

She knew that if she stood any chance at looking out for Baby Dom then she needed to come to some type of terms with Bruiser first. In a sense, she wanted to keep the peace.

She realized that although she never did anything to Bruiser, that Bruiser didn't see it that way.

Mystro needed to take the first step at peace, and she was ready.

When she walked into the rec room, she felt she would find Bruiser there but secretly hoped she'd be alone.

Deep down she knew that was a big wish because Bruiser was rarely ever alone.

Today was no different as her most loyal flunky, Cinnamon was there by her side. So, to her disappointment this conversation would have to be a trialogue.

"Aye, Bruiser, can I holla at you for a second?" Mystro asked.

Bruiser looked over at Mystro, rolled her eyes and continued to bounce the ball.

"Did you hear me Bruiser?" Mystro extended her neck and asked.

"She heard you, moe. Fuck you want?" Cinnamon replied.

Mystro cut her eyes toward her butt girl and stared back at Bruiser.

"Listen, I think you and I started things off on the wrong foot." Mystro continued. "We from the same city. And from what I can see, we like some of the same things so, let's just start over and try to get rid of some of this negative energy between us." Mystro propositioned.

Bruiser put the ball down near her foot and walked toward Mystro but stopped halfway.

"You know what, you may be right about us liking some of the same shit." Bruiser admitted.

Mystro nodded her head in agreement.

"The other day I woke up with a splitting headache. I never really get headaches, so I tried to figure out what was going on." Bruiser began.

Mystro shifted her weight from one foot to the other and changed the food container she held from her left to her right hand and continued to listen.

"You remember me bringing this shit up to you, Cinnamon?" She turned back and pointed her thumb towards her to ask.

"Yeah... Yeah." Bruiser's flunky replied.

"So, as I sat there with my head thumping wrecking my brain, for the life of me, only one thing came to mind." She looked Mystro up from feet to head. "You know what that was,

Myyystro?" Bruiser said drawing out her name.

Mystro was trying her best to be patient because she was extending the olive branch and didn't wanna show her disdain, but her nerves and tolerance were being tested.

"I can't say that I do." She replied dryly.

"I played the tapes back of my girl telling me that she knew you and your little friend. Then I started thinking about how she brought you up again when I talked to her on the phone shortly after our visit ended badly." Bruiser rubbed her chin.

"You mean after the visit ended because you hit her?" Mystro corrected.

"Oh, she going?" Cinnamon said.

Bruiser raised a hand to silence her friend. "Then my mind wandered to when I walked up on you at the phone banks and overheard your little conversation." She continued.

Mystro stood there waiting for more to be said because in the moment she was lost.

"Oh, so now you don't got nothing to say for yourself?" Bruiser asked.

"Aye, Bruiser, why I feel like every time we have a conversation you talk in parables? I can't decipher what you trying to say, so just say it." Mystro blurted out tired of the games.

Bruiser decided to ignore her statement for the moment.

She looked over at the container Mystro held in her hand.

"What you got there?" Bruiser asked.

"Oh, yeah, this the reason I came looking for you. When we were in the law library you were talking 'bout the crab cake egg rolls from back home." Mystro flipped the container around to open the lid. "It's virtually impossible to get good crab meat or even imitation crab meat in here. 'Specially in large quantities. But I was able to put in a order for some Jackfruit which is used to imitate crab meat in vegan dishes."

Mystro extended the container out towards Bruiser.

BY C. WASH

Cinnamon walked over to see what was inside.

"Jackfruit, the fuck?" Cinnamon laughed.

Bruiser looked over at her and smirked, displaying the dimple in her brown cheek.

"So, I improvised and made you what comes real close to crab cake egg rolls." Mystro continued. "They don't taste too bad either, especially when I added in my homemade crab sauce. Once I threw that together and put it there with some Old Bay, I couldn't tell the difference. Tastes just like home. I hope you like 'em." Mystro smiled proudly and waited for Bruiser to take the container out of her hand.

She didn't.

"Then my mind wandered back to your phone conversation that I walked up on last week." Bruiser picked up on the story as if she never paused while she walked closer to where Mystro stood.

Mystro brought the container back towards her body.

"I started to remember how you turned your back toward me once I approached. And how your conversation sounded real sexy and sweet. Then ended abruptly after I got on the phone."

Mystro was completely confused. "What are you talking–."

*"Damn, that sound good to me right about now. I sooooo can't wait to get home and get into that shit."* Bruiser repeated the conversation Mystro had with Native and now understood the confusion.

"Oh, no, Fam, it wasn't who you think. That was my–."

Bruiser snatched the container out of her hand, looked down at the food and spit in it before closing it back and shoving it into Mystro's stomach.

Mystro glared up at her.

She tried to make amends with Bruiser, but this fool was psychotic.

Mystro realized there was no reasoning with a lunatic.

132

"Look, I tried being cool with you, but now I see I'm just wasting my fucking time." Mystro replied.

"Fuck you and your time." Bruiser said, squaring up to Mystro.

Mystro threw the food container down and squared her body up to Bruiser. She dropped her right foot back to get into full fight stance. At this moment, it was whatever.

Before anything popped off, C.O. Michael walked into the rec room.

"Patterson! Your time is up in here. Let's go." He yelled.

Mystro didn't take her eyes off Bruiser.

She wasn't gonna throw the first punch but was still ready for whatever. Bruiser leaned in close.

"The next time I hear you talking to my girl on the phone I'm gonna break your motherfucking jaw so hard, you won't be able to talk to nobody for the rest of your life." She smirked as she stood back up straight.

"Patterson, if I call you out again you off rec for a week. Move!" C.O. Michael yelled out louder.

Mystro stood there on fire as Bruiser and Cinnamon walked out and didn't look back.

**BY C. WASH**

# CHAPTER TEN
# MYSTRO

**M**ystro was in the pantry area of the kitchen ingredients for her meal.

It had been a few days since the incident with Bruiser in the rec room but to Mystro, it felt like it happened yesterday.

She was still livid.

The fact that she went through a lot of trouble to re-create what Bruiser said she liked only to be disrespected, did not sit well with her. Sure, it wasn't crab meat. Even if it was, she was certain Bruiser would have found a way to hate it.

This was a power move.

And a disgusting one at that. Nah, she wouldn't take this lightly. She couldn't.

She needed to do something to show that she didn't appreciate that shit, but she would need help.

No worries.

She knew just who to talk to.

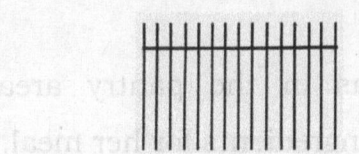

She could hear rain slapping at the walls outside of the prison, and it fit her mood. A storm was coming, and she would facilitate its move.

"Aye, Lo, how long would it take you to fulfill a special request order if I had one?" Mystro asked her cellmate Logan as she stood in front of her.

"I mean it really just depends on what I'm getting my hands on, sugar." Logan was sitting on her bunk looking at a magazine. "What is it?"

Mystro sighed.

Logan frowned. "Now you scaring me."

"Before I tell you, how do I know I can trust that what I asked for won't come back to bite me?" Mystro asked seriously.

"If you can't trust your celly you can't trust nobody." Logan joked.

Mystro gave her an all-knowing look. "This not a game."

"Yeah, ok, you gotta point." She said closing her magazine to give her full attention.

"But you gotta remember I'm on the line for this shit too." Logan advised. "If I snitch on you, it comes right back to me for smuggling stuff in."

Mystro nodded her head.

"So, no matter what it is and whatever you gonna do with it, on my kids, I wouldn't say nothing. Now what you need?" Logan reassured her.

"Sodium phosphate." Mystro said just above a whisper.

Logan looked puzzled and then as if a light bulb came on, she snapped her fingers and said, "laxative?"

Thunder clapped the sky.

"Yeah, in a manner of speaking." Mystro said in a low voice before she looked around.

"Oh, that shouldn't take me long at all, they got most of that stuff in the Infirmary. You know how this prison food can bind you up, no offense. A lot of bitches in here gotta take it when they ain't shittin'." Logan informed.

"Yeah, yeah I know but most of the time it's given as a prescription, and I need a lot of it." Mystro stepped closer. "A whole lot of it."

"That's still not a problem for me since it's in the facility I don't even have to send out for it." Logan said. "Just grease a few palms." She stood up. "After you grease mine."

"I can hit up my account. But when I do, how long?" Mystro asked with her eyes wide open.

"Give me two days."

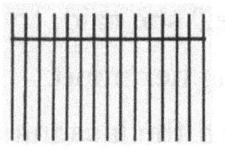

The cafeteria was bustling with laughs, shit talking and a few gripes. All that played in the background of Mystro's mind.

It was about to get serious.

Mystro stared down at the food trays in front of her. She needed privacy to do what she had to do next.

"Aye, can y'all start to load up the food into the service line for me please? I'll be right out." Mystro commanded.

"You got it, Cap." Chae said as she and the other kitchen workers grabbed the food trays and walked out into the dining area.

Now alone, Mystro walked to a separate warmer to get the food she made "special". She took a moment to look at the meal. It seemed innocent enough, but only she knew that it was far from the truth.

"It's go time," she said, trying to talk herself out of changing her mind.

She removed the lasagna and walked it out into the dining area.

Right on cue, she saw that Bruiser and Cinnamon were first in line to come eat.

*Greedy mothafuckas.* She thought.

They were always the first to come through to be served and Mystro was happy that today they were true to form.

While they grabbed their tan insulated food container trays, she walked up to the line and placed the lasagna down into the empty holder.

Next Mystro bopped over to the side of the salad bowl but made sure to keep her peripheral vision trained on the "special" lasagna.

This was a delicate situation as she only wanted to have Bruiser and Cinnamon eat from that tray and no one else.

As if they were in on the plan, Bruiser walked up to the line and had a chunk of lasagna placed onto her sectioned food container.

Her right hand, Cinnamon followed suit behind her and was dished up a serving of it as well. But before another inmate could get any put onto their container, Mystro walked toward the tainted lasagna holding a huge vat of steaming water.

She tripped and accidentally on purpose spilled all of it into the "special" dish.

"Oh, shit!" Mystro yelled out as the water splashed into the tray and caused the lasagna to spill out all over the place.

While the majority of the inmates laughed at Mystro's blunder, she smiled on the inside.

Her plan was coming together.

"Damn, my fault. Chae, serve the other lasagna while I get this cleaned up, please."

"P can serve, I'll go grab the mop." Chae said to Mystro.

"Clumsy ass dyke." Bruiser said out loud as she and Cinnamon continued to laugh on their way to the table to eat their dinner.

While Mystro assisted to clean up the mess she made, she beamed with excitement inside because she knew that soon, Bruiser wouldn't be able to find shit funny, literally.

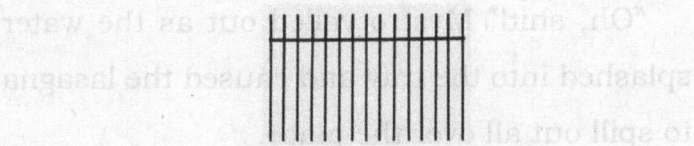

**TWO HOURS LATER**

The hallways boomed with regular commotion. Extra laughter at jokes that weren't really funny. Anger at unanswered calls.

But as if she was turning the dial to a radio station, Mystro was checking for something else.

Did her plan land?

BY C. WASH

She was antsy as she waited around for her experiment to take effect and was beginning to wonder if it would work.

But no sooner than she had the thought, she heard a bunch of commotion and laughter out on the block.

She got up off her bunk and pulled her white scrub shirt down over her tank top. Then walked to her cell door to see if it was what she thought.

As she sauntered out her cell and looked down onto the pod, she noticed a few inmates scattered throughout all looking and pointing to the left of the room.

She followed the direction they pointed in with her eyes and found the source of their amusement.

Cinnamon was curled up on the floor of the mouth of the bathroom door vomiting.

Mystro walked down the steps of the tier to get a closer look.

When she hit the last step, she saw what looked like a brown trail leading up to the bathroom.

As all the inmates in the entire pod looked in Cinnamon's direction. Mystro walked back to her cell with a smirk on her face.

In Mystro's mind, she won.

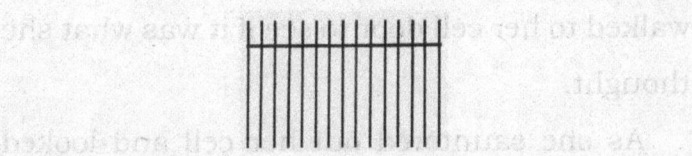

It had been some time, but curiosity got the best of Mystro. She needed to know that all shots met their target. And so, while everyone was in one direction, she went to the other.

A bathroom she knew Bruiser preferred.

Mystro pushed forward on a mission.

Slowly she walked toward the stall where Bruiser was shitting her brains out.

Moans rung in the air.

"Oh my God! What the fuck did I eat?" Bruiser said as she sharted into the toilet bowl.

Without saying a word, Mystro glided up to the stall where another brown trail stopped and slid the food container with the egg rolls that Bruiser spat into, under the door.

*"Checkmate, bamma ass nigga."* Mystro said to herself as she dipped out the bathroom smiling.

# CHAPTER ELEVEN
## MYSTRO

**M**ystro wanted to go and check on Baby Dom. She needed to make sure she was cool and felt it was the perfect time to do so as she knew that Bruiser would be in the infirmary.

She walked into the unlocked cell and noticed that Baby Dom was lying on her bunk.

"Aye, BD can I holla at you for a second?" Mystro asked as she walked into the cell and shut the door behind herself.

Baby Dom quickly turned her body over and noticed Mystro.

She jumped off the top bunk.

"Aye, fam what...what you doing here?" Baby Dom asked while looking behind her at the door.

"I came to talk to you. But fuck all that, what's wrong with your eye?" Mystro questioned angrily.

"Oh, nah, this nothing just...just bumped into something that's all. How you been man? I miss you, My." Baby Dom answered in an attempt to avoid the subject.

"Bumped into something? Hell nah! That shit look like somebody hit you. The fuck, Baby Dom?" Mystro snapped.

"Chill, Mystro I don't want us to get in trouble." Baby Dom replied.

"Get in trouble with who? I can be in here. I know you not talking about Bruiser. Is that what you mean?" Mystro rambled.

"Yes. She don't like people in here when she not here so maybe we should go to your crib." Baby Dom said nervously as she looked over Mystro's shoulder.

"First of all, don't even trip off her. She not coming back no time soon. She in the infirmary, I saw to that." Mystro admitted proudly.

"That was you?" Baby Dom asked, shocked.

147

"Yeah, but keep that shit on the low." Mystro informed.

Baby Dom nodded so fast she looked like she had a bobble head.

"I ain't wanna believe what I heard about her possibly fucking with you in here, but it looks like nigga's was right. So, I gave her a taste of her own medicine so to speak."

"Oh no."

"What?"

"You think...you think she gonna find out?" Baby Dom asked nervously.

Of course she would find out. Mystro saw to it.

"Don't worry, folks don't mess with people that control their food. She not gonna fuck with you no more. I can promise you that." Mystro reassured her.

Baby Dom sighed in relief.

"Thank you, fam. Slim been giving me all kinds of trouble. I never even did nothing to her. I'm so glad you here for me and I'm sorry I--"

148

"Nah, Baby Dom, you don't have to apologize for nothing. Truth be told, it's me who actually needs to come up off the sorry's." Mystro admitted.

Baby Dom sat down on Bruiser's bunk and listened.

"Ever since I got here my whole focus has been leaving this place and when I saw you come into this prison, it just put everything into perspective." Mystro took a deep breath.

Baby Dom looked down in shame. "I'm sorry I put this on you."

"Just listen, kid. Let me push this out."

Baby Dom nodded.

"All that shit really did go down and now both of us are locked up. I didn't wanna have to look out for *you and me*, but that was wrong." Mystro walked up closer to Baby Dom. "We peoples and I should've never tried to make you deny that shit." Mystro sat down next to Baby Dom. "I mean you in here for me and I owe you my life." Mystro confessed looking into Baby Dom's good and bad eye.

"It's cool, bro you know I would do that shit all over again if I had to." Baby Dom smiled at Mystro.

Mystro laughed. "Your crazy lil ass probably would."

"Stamp." Baby Dom smiled.

The two embraced in a one arm hug.

And while they made up on the forbidden Bruiser's bed, she looked on intensely from outside the cell.

BY C. WASH

# CHAPTER TWELVE
## MYSTRO

Shit was too quiet as Mystro walked through the corridor on her way to the kitchen.

Her antennas were raised.

Bruiser was in the hallway talking with two other inmates when they spotted her. Mystro saw them and although she didn't feel like dealing with any mouth from Bruiser, she knew she couldn't turn around and avoid her.

She was in her head about the talk that her and Baby Dom had and how she could come up with a way to have her lawyer look at her case to see if there was any way her sentence could also be reduced.

Had she not been in her head, she would have noticed them a lot sooner and been able to change direction before they saw her, but now it was too late.

She proceeded to bypass the women and was almost past when she felt her body being lifted off the ground in one swift motion.

Before she could react, she found herself snatched into the chapel of the facility surrounded by Bruiser, and the two other inmates whom she was not familiar with but would never forget.

Mystro said, "The fuck is-"

"Yeah, hold up on all that shit." Bruiser cut her off and started. "Before you get into a whole question session, let me take you straight to the answers." She continued.

Mystro straightened out her prison uni and eye balled all three of them.

"That shit you pulled with my food was cute. You lucky all it did was cause me a little stomach ache and diarrhea. Some short shit I could get over. But now you gotta pay." Bruiser stated.

"Slim, I don't even know what you talking 'bout." Mystro denied all knowledge of the laxative events. "But it seems to me if someone did something to your food, it may have been because of something you started in the first place."

"Bitch, is you stupid or just crazy?" Bruiser said. "You came into the stall and all but took responsibility! You think you real cute don't you, dyke?" Bruiser asked.

"Nah, but apparently your girl does." Mystro chuckled.

Bruiser stared at Mystro for longer than necessary and then smiled.

She tore her eyes away from Mystro and gave the other two inmates an all-knowing look.

"Yeah, aight then. I'ma leave y'all to it. Besides, when this gets out, I need to have been seen somewhere else." Bruiser said before she winked at Mystro and walked out the chapel door.

What was about to happen?

She finally got it.

Mystro squared up to face the two inmates who remained behind.

"Oh, I get it, y'all 'sposed to put in the body work, huh? In her name?" Mystro chuckled once although wasn't shit funny. "How could y'all even fuck with a nigga like her?" She asked them.

"Yo, we don't get involved in all that. We get paid to do a job and that's what we gonna do." Chocolate Medium Thick inmate stated.

Mystro quickly scanned her surroundings to make note of what she could use to her advantage in this fight if need be.

Mystro said, "Well, I guess you gotta do what you gotta-"

WOOSH.

Tall Boney inmate swung on Mystro but she ducked the blow and came back with an upper cut to her chin with the back of her head.

"Arrrggggghhhhhh!" Boney cried out.

This sent Medium Thick inmate into activation mode, and she stole Mystro in the mouth with a strong left jab.

It stung, but Mystro ate it and came back with a right jab of her own.

It rocked the chin of Medium Thick and Mystro followed up with a quick left hook that dropped her to her knees.

Mystro shuffled her feet and was squared up and ready for whatever Tall Boney was gonna do.

"What's up?" Mystro yelled out.

Tall Boney shook her head to try and regain her composure but Mystro ain't no dummy and this wasn't no boxing ring.

Instead of waiting to play defense, Mystro attacked.

Hard.

She threw two stiff body blows to the torso of Tall Boney and once she bent over in pain, Mystro worked her face over.

After she threw so many combination punches that both of her opponents were on the ground, she dropped her shoulders and looked at them.

It was almost too easy if she was being honest.

"Next time, tell that bitch to handle her own business!" Mystro declared out of breath before she stepped over them and proceeded with business as usual to the kitchen.

# CHAPTER THIRTEEN
## NATIVE

The fall wind whipped the leaves around Native's car as she sat in the driver's seat in heavy thought contemplating her next move.

"Before she could make a decision her phone rang.

*"You have a collect call from... Mystro. An inmate at Washington Alley Prison. Do you accept the charges?"*

"Of course...Mystro, what's good?" Native questioned, hitting the speaker icon on her cell.

"Son, you would not believe the crazy shit that's popped off since I last talked to you. What you doing?" Mystro asked, taking a deep breath. Being sure to check her surroundings.

"Truthfully, sitting here debating on whether or not I'm going inside this bar to get drunk." Native looked out of the windshield of her car at the neon lights flashing on the building.

"This early? What's up, man everything good?" Mystro blinked and raised her eyebrows with concern.

"Mystro, I don't even know anymore. This living together shit with Brisa is stressing me out. I don't think I'm built for it." Native leaned back in the seat and the leather moaned.

"Damn," Mystro sighed. "Not to make light of your shit but I wish I could only stress off of living with a broad right about now."

"Oh, yeah right, 'cuz that worked out so well with you before." Native said sarcastically referring to her and Church.

Mystro smirked.

"Point taken. I can't believe she fucking with your mental like that. I would have never seen that shit coming." Mystro admitted.

"Me either! But I'ma get through it. Shit, or I'ma have to dip, for real for real." Native convinced herself sitting back up. "What's up, man? What's going on there?"

"Slim, you remember that little situation I told you about and the advice you gave me?"

"Absolutely."

"Well, I listened to you. Tried to squash everything and got Shawty back in the fold. But this SW, you remember from your last visit here right." Mystro used slang and code for whomever was possibly listening to try and shield the fact that she was speaking about Bruiser.

"Oh, yeah, bamma dyke from down the wharf with shawty, that kept staring." Native recalled.

"Exactly! Slim is making major problems for a nigga." Mystro said in a sharp tone.

"Major problems like what? Some shit that might get you hemmed up?"

"Yeah, that among other things. Fam, I need you to go ahead and come on a visit so I can tell you what's going on face-to-face. You know I can't get into too many details on this phone." Mystro reminded her.

Since they did talk about some shit over the phone before, Native realized this was even more serious. "I got you. Consider me there."

Mystro sighed in relief.

"Aye, young, in the meantime make sure you remain on task." Native schooled. "I don't know what's going on, but I know you can't risk not being able to come home. This is where you belong, fam." Native took a deep breath.

"Facts." Mystro nodded her head.

"I can hear that you frustrated through this phone and I know you the kind of nigga that has the ability to snap. I mean, case in

160

point, look where you at." Native reminded her.

Mystro sighed.

"No matter what's happening, all that shit is temporary, Fammo. Trust me. Don't do something that you gonna regret and not be able to come home sooner than later." Native said sternly.

"My nigga, I hear you. Believe me I hear you, but you have no idea what it's like in here. Add on the fact that now it's not just me that I gotta look out for. I feel like I'm about to lose it." Mystro confessed.

"Aye man, you remember when we was living at the house and the only thing we was tripping off of was making sure we had the rent money for Margaret?"

Mystro laughed once.

"Sometimes I sit back and think about those days and wish I could go right back there." Native put her head down and smiled.

"Yeah, simpler times." Mystro ran her hand through her hair. "Man, I swear to God, I wish I would have never left there." She admitted. "Shit getting weird as fuck."

"Look, son, I'll be there this weekend. I promise you but don't do nothing you gonna regret. I need you back here, my nigga. I need you back home. Promise me, My."

"I don't wanna lie to you, Native so I'm not going to promise you but I will think hard about all my moves before I make any." Mystro said honestly.

"Aye, fam, when all else fails. Pray."

"Same, bro...same."

# CHAPTER FOURTEEN
# MYSTRO

Mystro paced back and forth in her cell. Shit was getting serious, and she found herself working out all of Bruiser's next steps, even though she couldn't have possibly known what the jailhouse butch was about to do next.

She was uneasy and tense and the pacing helped her to think. But she wanted to remain calm. She knew if she was calm, she could think two steps ahead.

At least she hoped.

"Open seven!" C.O. Michael stood in front of the door and yelled to unlock Mystro's cell.

When the door popped, Michael walked in to see Mystro in the middle of the room.

"Mason, what's going on?" C.O. Michael asked Mystro as he stood in the doorway.

Mystro shook her head and tried to put on a fake smile.

"Nothing, just thinking. You need something?"

C.O. Michael walked into the cell completely and pulled the door closed for privacy which made Mystro a little uneasy.

A closed door with just a C.O. and an inmate was unorthodox.

"What's going on, C.O.?" Mystro asked puzzled. "You got me worried."

"I need to say something for just your ears only." He informed.

Mystro was still on pause but curious.

"Look, I know you and Patterson got into it and from what I can see, y'all still going at it."

"Oh, nah, what you came in on the other day was just shit talk over basketball. Nothing serious." Mystro lied.

"I'm not talking about that." He waved the air. "I know y'all got beef and it seems to be escalating." He continued.

Mystro didn't show any signs of C.O. Michael telling the truth. She wanted to just listen and not give herself up in any way.

After all, he was still police.

"Look, you don't have to confirm or deny anything, but I need you to hear what I'm saying to you." C.O. Michael walked up closer to Mystro.

Mystro didn't move.

"Patterson's been in here and will be in here for a very long time." He started. "I'm sure if the day came and she ever got released she'd be right back down here within a month. If that long. I've seen this shit with her type, time and time again." He informed.

Mystro's shoulders dropped as she began to relax.

"But you different, Mystro." C.O. Michael stated. He softly touched her shoulder.

Mystro stood erect again.

"You got a bright future in front of you but that won't matter if you're stuck in this prison." He stressed.

Mystro sighed and walked toward her bunk to sit down. He officially softened her heart for the moment anyway.

"Don't let Patterson or any other inmate get into your head. You've been doing so well staying clear of shit. Do not let this prison pull you under."

"Listen, C.O., I'm not sure what you talking about. All I do is cook and do my time. I'm not mixed into whatever is going on with Bruiser."

C.O. Michael sighed and squatted down so he was on eye level with Mystro.

"I feel partially responsible for the drama because I put you down about what was happening with her and your friend." He sighed. "So, for that, if I can help you in any way, I will." C.O. Michael looked into Mystro's eyes and told her sincerely. "But you have to be careful. You have to be cautious. And you

166

have to watch your back more than you ever have in your life."

Although she felt like he was being genuine, he was still a C.O. so, she needed to tread lightly.

"Thank you for your concern and your advice, but I'm cool. No need to worry. I'm good."

# CHAPTER FIFTEEN
# MYSTRO

**M**ystro and Native sat across from one another in the visiting hall. It was semi-crowded as visitation had just opened back up and everyone wanted to see their loved ones.

For some reason Mystro was focused on a kid who was eating the vending machine wings and she wondered why they didn't just buy him McDonalds.

"Son, is you listening?" Native said, jogging her out of her thoughts.

"Oh, yeah..."

"And so I'm sitting there after my third shot of Casamigos and I'm jive contemplating a fourth." Native was recanting her evening at the bar for Mystro.

Mystro, who was physically present, was slumped down in her chair and seemed distant and uninterested.

"The broad who was slinging the tequila was fire, too. I was about to, yeah, you feel me?" Native continued.

"Mm hmm," Mystro replied dryly. She crossed her arms over her chest.

"But then my fucking phone got to ringing. So, I looked at it or whatever and it was Bri, blowing my shit up!" Native sat back in her seat dramatically as she recanted the events of the other night.

"Next thing I know, she walked her ass into the damn bar! On some lunatic shit! Yoouunnggg, I was heated." For the first time since Native started the story, Mystro looked at her.

She didn't say anything but Native had her attention.

"Aye, son, what the fuck is your issue?" Native asked.

"What?" Mystro said.

"I'm here, I'm telling you how twisted up my shit is and you sitting there like I ate your lunch or something. The fuck!" Native asked, slapping the table once.

"Why you in here running off about your love life? I told you I had some serious shit I'm going through. I feel like I'm about to kirk out."

"Aight, that's why I came. So we can talk this shit out, but you don't gotta carry me while I'm telling you what I'm going through either, slim." Native shot back.

Mystro took a deep breath and sat up straighter.

She ran her hand down her face.

"That's fair. My bad, son. This whole situation has my mind warped, but you right. What happened when she came through?" Mystro asked.

"Nigga, she came straight to the bar and for my throat." Native threw her hands up and explained. "Got to going, talking about why you ain't picked up your phone and who you in here with. It was non-stop."

BY C. WASH

"But that's your brand, you know you like 'em a little crazy." Mystro reminded her.

"I'm hip, that was my move back in the day. But I ain't sign up for that with shawty. She wasn't giving off none of those vibes before we signed that lease."

Mystro chuckled.

"Yeah, but I bet you strapped the shit outta her that night though, right?" Mystro questioned.

Native was quiet. She lifted up the black skull cap she wore and scratched her head.

She looked down at the snacks on the table and picked up a cold hot wing and took a bite. Just like the kid.

"I'm right, ain't I?" Mystro persisted as she waited for her answer.

"Don't act like you know me, nigga!" Native smirked. "So what got you so fired up?" She dropped the chicken bones onto the napkin.

Mystro sat up and scooted closer to Native to shield what she wanted to say from others.

"That bamma ass broad over there is gunning for me, young. And the shit has gotten out of control." Mystro cut her eyes across the room to where Bruiser and her girlfriend sat.

Native wanted to look too but didn't wanna be hot. After all, the last time the four of them were in a room together, visitations were cut. So she picked up a paper towel and wiped her fingers instead.

"She tried to have me jumped, slim." Mystro informed barely moving her lips.

Native put the paper towel down and scooted her chair closer to the table. She couldn't believe her ears. She cut her eyes across to the corner of the room while her head remained down.

"That's where you got that cut on your lip from?" Native asked just above a whisper.

BY C. WASH

"Yeah," Mystro scanned the room before she continued. "They snatched me into the chapel and tried to work me."

Native chuckled. "But I bet they ain't know they was squaring up with "The Natural" did they?" Native said referring to Mystro's former boxing nickname.

"Nah, they found out real quick though."

Native grabbed her bottled water and sat back. "How many?"

"At first it was slim and two others, but before blows were thrown, slim dipped." Mystro said explaining how Bruiser left before the fight started. Only to miss her folks getting their asses whooped.

"Alibi?" Native insinuated.

"Exactly. But shit ain't play in her favor though." Mystro continued.

"Of course it didn't. So now what?" Native asked. She took a sip of her water.

"What you mean? I gotta get this bamma back." Mystro stated with raised eyebrows.

"Wrong!" Native said as she shook her head from left to right and closed her eyes.

Mystro glared.

"You gotta come home, fam. Look, she not gonna try nothing else. More than likely she gonna stay on guard thinking you gonna come back at her." Native shrugged her shoulders and explained.

"I don't know, Nae. This bamma different. She get an idea in her head and start lunching." Mystro replied.

"Nah, trust me, I know bitches like her." Native advised.

"I keep telling you prison is different."

"Hear me out." Native leaned closer. "She took her shot and she missed badly. She not gonna do shit else unless you kick it back up. Let that shit ride and stay out the heat." Native warned.

Mystro took a deep breath and her nostrils flared.

"What you huffing and puffing about?" Native asked.

174

"I got into this bullshit in the first place looking out for Baby Dom. Which you told me I had to do by the way, but you not trying to even see what I'm dealing with or give me sound advice on what to do now." Mystro explained.

"I am telling you what to do!" Native said back in a harsh tone just above a whisper. "Keeping this beef going at this point is dumb." Native continued.

Mystro snatched her grape soda off the table and sat back.

"You don't get it. It ain't like that in here man. This ain't out in the streets."

"If you ask me it sounds just like 'em." Native said. "But since you feel like you gotta do something else, what you thinking 'bout doing?"

"I don't know, that's my problem. But I gotta strike back. I'm just not sure how." Mystro admitted. She took a gulp of her soda.

"Well, since you say I put you in this shit, let me help you out." Native said with an attitude.

She put her water bottle down on the table and got up from her seat.

Mystro's eyes widened. "What you doing?"

Native brushed her jeans off and cut her eyes towards Mystro before she walked away from her.

"Where you going, slim?" Mystro repeated, puzzled.

Native didn't reply. Just kept walking.

As Mystro watched closely, she saw Native head over toward Bruiser and her girlfriend's table.

Mystro raised her eyebrows as she looked on intensely to see what played out. She felt dizzy and she was so confused. After all, this could've went a million different ways.

As if she were watching a movie, she saw Native bend down and whisper into The Girlfriend's ear. All while Bruiser looked on in confusion.

**176**

"What the fuck is you doing?" Bruiser shot up and yelled.

The girlfriend smiled and then immediately turned her smile into a forced scowl.

Native stood straight up and sauntered back toward her and Mystro's table to gather her things.

The room erupted in chatter and laughs.

"Mason!" C.O. Michael yelled out. "Your visit is over! Line up!"

"The fuck was that?" Mystro stood up with her arms and hands open and said.

"Now, you got her back, happy?" Native asked sarcastically.

While the laughter in the hall continued, Native adjusted her hat and walked to the door.

Mystro and Bruiser on the other hand just glared at each other from across the room.

# CHAPTER SIXTEEN
# BABY DOM
# ONE MONTH LATER

**B**aby Dom lie on her bunk in deep thought. She reflected on her life and what it had shaped up to become. She never had a true family. Growing up she bounced from one foster home to the next.

Her last foster mother only wanted to collect a check and did not care what Baby Dom did in the streets just as long as she was home when the social worker came.

This left her plenty of time to be wild, that is until she met Mystro and Native.

She thought they were the coolest Dom's in DC and wanted nothing more than to be friends. To be in their worlds.

It worked out better than that as they took to Baby Dom like family.

BY C. WASH

While she stared at the picture of Native, Mystro and herself, Bruiser and Cinnamon walked into the cell.

In the past couple of weeks, she had become the personal servant to Bruiser. With no let up.

It appeared that Bruiser no longer went after Mystro and decided to take all her frustrations out on Baby Dom directly.

She also made Baby Dom totally ignore Mystro. She told her if she caught her so much as looking at Mystro, she would kill her.

Baby Dom didn't know how serious she was but didn't want to risk her friend being killed.

It hurt her heart when she had to tell Mystro that she didn't want to be bothered and to leave her alone when approached by one of her closest friends.

Mystro couldn't wrap her head around it and began to think something else was up but eventually decided to give Baby Dom her space.

Now, without her friend, Baby Dom wondered if it was all worth it.

"Hold up...Why you ain't done folding my shit up yet, Baby Dyke?" Bruiser yelled as she and Cinnamon walked into the cell pulling Baby Dom out of her thoughts.

"Oh, nah, I still got a little to go but, I promise, it won't take me long." Baby Dom turned her body over and stated.

"Well hurry your young ass up! You should've been done. It wasn't nothing but two weeks worth of laundry."

Baby Dom looked mad but didn't say anything else, just began to fold the clothes faster.

"Homie, you loafing. How you gonna have this kid fluffing and folding your dirty draws and shit?" Cinnamon asked.

"'Cuz that's how it is in here. Nothing's free, not even sharing this cell. Gotta pull your weight." Bruiser shot back. "Besides, she gotta debt she gotta work off. As a matter of fact...Put them clothes down and come over here and clean my slide."

Baby Dom put down the huge draws she was attempting to fold. "What you say? I ain't hear you." She asked.

"Oh, you heard me youngin'! Get yo ass over here and clean this spot off my fucking shoe."

Baby Dom walked over to where the women stood.

Her body was tense.

When she was in front of them she slowly bent down and held out her hand for Bruiser to take her shoe off and give it to her.

"Nah, get yo ass down on your knees and clean it off while it's still on my foot." Bruiser laughed.

Baby Dom stood back up and looked around the cell for the rag she used to clean up. When she spotted it, she walked around the women and grabbed it before going to work.

"Watch this shit." Bruiser whispered to Cinnamon before focusing back on Baby Dom.

Like a robot, Baby Dom came back and faced the women again.

Bruiser sat down on the bottom bunk and stretched out her long legs dramatically.

Baby Dom bent down again to grab the slide off her foot. She was beginning to get extremely pissed.

"Leave it on. Get on your knees and lick them shits clean." Bruiser demanded while looking up at her friend, Cinnamon.

Baby Dom stood back up straight. "Hold up. What you mean?" She asked, confused.

"Fuck is you hard of hearing?" Bruiser yelled. "I said don't use that rag, get down on your knees and use your tongue instead." She restated.

Baby Dom stared at her for longer than she should have. She took a minute to assess her predicament. She cut her eyes to Cinnamon who was standing to her left. She slowly looked back down at Bruiser.

Her spirit was defeated.

Even if she wanted to swell up her chest to try and take on Bruiser, she knew it would be in vain as Cinnamon was right there. She figured the moment she swung on her Cinnamon would pound her into the floor of the cell.

But fuck it, she was sick of this bitch.

Baby Dom had time today.

"Man, I'm not 'bout to lick no shit off your shoe." Baby Dom yelled having had enough.

Cinnamon laughed before Bruiser cut her a look so cold she stopped in mid chuckle.

"Fuck you just say to me?" Bruiser asked.

"Man, I said-"

Before Baby Dom could finish her statement Bruiser hopped up from the bunk and stole Baby Dom in the face twice.

Baby Dom stumbled back into Cinnamon who caught her then threw her down to the floor.

**183**

Bruiser hovered over top of Baby Dom who blinked rapidly trying to see around the blood gushing out of her eye. She looked at her knuckles and shook her hand to relieve the pain.

"Damn, my fucking knuckle gonna be swollen. This why I pay niggas to handle my work." Bruiser said looking at her fingers. "Now, lick that shit off my slide." She demanded. "And if you get blood or tears on 'em, I'm gonna fuck your ass up even more."

**BY C. WASH**

# CHAPTER SEVENTEEN
## NATIVE

Native didn't know what Brisa thought she was doing but cooking wasn't it.

The eggs were cold and hard.

The toast was nothing more than stale bread and the bacon smelled as if it died and came back twice.

The best thing about this breakfast was the fresh coffee that she herself made earlier.

Native wasn't concerned about eating anyway so it didn't matter. The only thing on her mind was the email she was reading from Mystro, which gave her anxiety.

Although rarely utilized, she was happy they set up this option to communicate via the prison, and she wouldn't forget it again.

But she could already since by the tone and exclamation points that things weren't going as planned.

Baby Dom was supposed to be protected. But it looked like Mystro had dropped the ball.

*Native,*

*You probably don't wanna read this! To be honest I had trouble writing it. Me venting to you about what was popping off wasn't a reason for you to do what you did. I just needed feedback. But I'm sure you'll think it was what I wanted. That wasn't the case!*

*But this ain't about all that! It's about something else!*

*After you left, I seen a change in Baby Dom. At first I thought it was her lunching, like she normally does especially when she can't get her way. But this is different. A few of the broads that know me around here and know we were cool said they were concerned.*

*When I asked about what, they led me to believe that she could possibly be doing something else. And since my emails are probably read by the staff, I can't go into detail. But what I will say is this, remember that broad 'round the way?*

*The one with the white mother and Asian father? Who claimed she wasn't mixed when she was?*

*You remember what she used to do when she thought nobody was listening? Nobody was watching?*

*That's what I believe is going on now.*

Native looked up for a second to catch her breath.

The chick who she was speaking about who looked Asian even though she said she wasn't, was an addict. At one point she would lace her weed with crack but when she wanted a bigger high she would shoot up instead.

Native knew this couldn't be the case. After all, Baby Dom moved smarter than this.

Or did she?

She took a huge gulp of her coffee.

Focusing back on the email, she decided to finish.

*I tried to pull her over to the side a few times and speak to her. But she called herself carrying me. I never wanted her here, man! I told you this shit before! She made the decision to come anyway.*

*But I guess you think that's my fault too right?!!!!*

*Anyway, I just figured I'd let you know. This ain't no call for us to get back cool again.*

*At least not before you apologize.*

Native sucked her teeth and slid her iPad across the table.

Apologize for what to hear her tell it?

Mystro orchestrated this drama in Native's mind.

Yeah, she had no business walking up to the girl and doing what she did, but she felt she needed to prove to Mystro that retaliation

would only make shit worse. Almost wanted
her to make the move.

But none of that mattered.

Too much time had passed.

The only thing on her mind now was
finding out if Baby Dom was okay.

But how?

# CHAPTER EIGHTEEN
# MYSTRO

Mystro was on fire. She was so angry she couldn't see straight.

After reading her reply email and seeing Native blame her for everything that was going on she felt that once again she didn't understand what she was going through.

After all she was the one that was doing time. She was the one that would possibly be locked up for a big chunk of her life.

And if Native was truly the homie she would get where she was coming from. What was the fucking problem?

Mystro walked up to the phone, snatched the handset and dialed the numbers.

Before Native could add the ... "LLO" to the "He", Mystro laid into her.

"So you blaming *me* for this shit!" She yelled into the receiver. Her nose flared.

"What you talking about, Mystro?" Native asked.

"Hold up, you send me an email and now you don't know what the fuck I'm talking about?" Mystro asked, confused.

"I sent you the email because I knew you would do exactly what you doing! But since you finally called and stopped acting like a fucking kid, let me tell you what's on my mind." Native paused. "If that girl dies in there this is on your head."

Mystro felt like she had been dropped down an elevator shaft.

"Man, how the fuck is this shit on me?" She gritted her teeth and her temple vein bulged.

"Are you really asking me that question, champ?" Native asked.

"Yes!" Mystro yelled. "I mean I know that I was on some different shit when she got here 'cuz I was in my feelings, but I made shit right. I can't even run down all the shit I did to make sure slim was cool!" She looked around to ensure no one was ear hustling.

"Nigga, no you haven't! If you had, you would have never sent me no email like that. You was just trying to settle your guilt." Native called her out.

Mystro felt gut punched.

"That's how you really feel, son?" Mystro asked now with sadness in her eyes.

"Man, I'm done playing games with you. I said what I said. She's your responsibility. And since we both come from fucked up backgrounds, she's one of the only family members we got left. I don't know what you got to do but you better help her get back to who she is. Or else."

Click.

Mystro was beyond livid.

Not because Native went off on her.

But because she spoke the truth.

For some reason, now her anger was directed at Baby Dom.

She hadn't said anything else to her since she last saw her over two weeks ago. After all she made several attempts to help her but Baby Dom refused to even give her any rap.

But now she was causing a beef between her and her oldest friend.

Mystro walked with purpose towards her cell, ready to let Baby Dom have it, but what she saw next put her on pause.

Baby Dom was on all fours in the corner of the cell licking Bruiser's slide like a dog.

Not only was Bruiser laughing hard on the floor clutching her stomach as if she was in pain but Cinnamon, who was also in there, laughed too.

Like them two clowns wasn't just in the middle of the tier shitting and throwing up all over themselves a while back.

But it was the blank stare in Baby Dom's eyes that made Mystro turn white.

There was no laughter.

There was no joy.

There was no humanity.

She was only a shell of the person that she once knew.

And that hit different.

Deeper.

And in a way that Mystro would never be able to come back from.

On some superhero shit, Mystro stormed into the cell and snatched Baby Dom by the forearm. As she yoked her towards the exit, Bruiser stepped up as if to stop her. But the look in Mystro's eyes told her now was not the fucking time. Unless she wanted to be dropped.

Once they were out in the hallway of the tier Baby Dom shoved Mystro back.

"Get off me!" Baby Dom looked at her as if she didn't know her.

"You in there licking a nigga's shoe with your eye all wrapped up and you telling me to get off you? What's wrong with you, slim?" Mystro yelled down into Baby Dom's face.

194

"You said you don't fuck with me remember?" She asked, as if tears were rising but she was pressing them down. "That you didn't want nothing to do with me."

"BD, why you bringing up old shit? I told you I was lunching when you first got in here. But that was then, I didn't mean--"

"Then or now it don't matter, you showed how you felt about me, for real for real. Now I want *you* to leave *me* alone and stay the fuck out my life!" She yelled before she stormed back into the cell.

HERSBAND MATERIAL 2: JAILHOUSE BUTCH

# CHAPTER NINETEEN
## MYSTRO

It was quiet on the tier where Mystro stayed.

Unusually quiet for this time of day, but the inmates had received their store orders earlier, so most of them were in their cells eating, reading or flipping their clits.

Mystro knew she needed to do something to try and help Baby Dom, no matter what she said, but she also knew she couldn't do it on her own. So she decided to see if what C.O. Michael told her, when he said he would help her, was real.

"Wow, who eats sushi and egg salad? Like really that's what you brought in here?" Mystro said as she approached the security desk on the lower level of her tier.

"Tastes good to me," he burped.

"You ain't gotta eat that struggle meal, you know I would have whipped something up for you if you needed me to." She joked.

"Oh really?" He smiled and put his spork down.

Mystro nodded, still holding her nose. "Shit smells foul."

"You ever had this combination? It's the best you'll ever taste, trust me." C.O. Michael defended his choices.

"I'll take your word for it." Mystro said as she sat on the bench near the desk.

"What's up, Mason, what you need?" C.O. Michael wiped his mouth and asked.

"Um," Mystro paused.

She stood up and walked in closer to the desk. "Can I talk to you privately?" She asked.

C.O. Michael looked around before he answered. "Sure, meet me in the kitchen."

Five minutes later Mystro and C.O. Michael were in the kitchen alone.

C.O. Michael sat up on the counter and waited for Mystro to ask for what she needed.

"Look I know it's unconventional for me to be coming at you like this but I'm desperate."

"Get to the point, Mason. I prefer it that way."

She nodded. "Okay, uh, were you serious when you said you'd help me? Because I need you."

C.O. Michael smiled.

## BABY DOM

Baby Dom was alone in her cell lying face up on her bunk as she stared at the ceiling.

She hadn't left her cell all day which was becoming her norm.

Not to eat, not to shower or do anything else.

At the moment Bruiser was nowhere in sight but was never too far away.

The cell door buzzed open.

"Dent," C.O. Michael called out. "Roll up your bunk! You moving." He commanded. He stood in the doorway and waited for her.

For the first time all day, Baby Dom sat up and looked at the door.

"Where am I moving to?" She asked.

"Just roll up your bunk! I'll let you know when we get there." He replied booming with authority.

Baby Dom eased off her bed and began to gather her things slowly. She moved like a person who didn't care about anything anymore.

Then she paused her movement and her eyes roamed back and forth like she watched something only she could see.

"Does this have anything to do with Mystro?" She asked looking up at C.O. Michael.

"What, inmate?" He questioned.

"Does me moving have anything to do with Mystro?" Baby Dom asked again before she grabbed another item.

He was puzzled why she would even ask. In his opinion, she should be happy to move out of the cell with Bruiser, no matter where she ended up.

"Yeah, you moving in with Mason. What difference does it make? Just pack your shit." He advised.

Baby Dom stood motionless. "No."

"What you say?"

"Nah." Baby Dom said as she climbed back on her bunk and lied back down.

"Dent, what the fuck you doing? I said let's go." C.O. Michael barked forcefully.

"With all due respect, I'm just gonna stay right here." She said as she stared up at the ceiling. "Thanks."

C.O. Michael stood there stuck but came to the realization that if she didn't wanna move, he couldn't make her. Especially not

for a favor. But he still wanted to make sure
he did all he could to help Mystro.

So he tried one last time.

"Dent, I'm not gonna ask you again, this is
your last shot, what's it gonna be?" He asked
with both of his hands resting on his belt.

"I'm good." She replied before she rolled
over and closed her eyes.

# CHAPTER TWENTY
## MYSTRO

Mystro paced in her cell back and forth anxiously.

Because she frequently paced, it was a wonder there wasn't a path worn out in the concrete.

When she saw C.O. Michael coming up onto her tier, she raced to the door.

"So, what happened?" She asked as soon as it opened.

"You tell me." Her current cellmate Logan said as she walked into their cell.

"Oh, Logan, I thought you were someone else." She said as she looked over top of Logan's head and sighed.

"Nah, it's just me, you know, your cellmate. At least I thought I was your cellmate." She said sarcastically.

"What's that supposed to mean?" Mystro asked.

**BY C. WASH**

"How come I had to hear that you requested a new celly? Why you just ain't come to me?" Logan asked as she sat on Mystro's bunk and swept her braids over her shoulder.

Prison was worse than high school with the gossip shit. Once something went down, it didn't take long for it to get all over the block.

"Lo, it's not you and it wasn't just a new celly." Mystro explained. "You know Baby Dom?"

"Yeah, Lil yo in Bruiser's cell, right?" Logan replied.

"Yeah, well that's my homie from 'round the way and I was trying to get her in here with me." Mystro continued. "Bruiser is putting her through it down there and I can't just get her moved, I gotta get her with me so I can look out for her."

Logan shook her head slowly. "But I don't wanna go up in there with her either!" Logan replied.

"Lo, she not gonna fuck with you like she doing Baby Dom. The only reason she messing with her is 'cuz she new, younger and my folks." Mystro explained.

"Oh, I'm not worried about her fucking with me, but she nasty, Mystro. I ain't trying to live like that." Logan confessed.

Mystro understood her concern. She knew firsthand that shawty was trifling.

"Aight, so how 'bout this, I try and make arrangements for Cinnamon to move in there with Bruiser and you go downstairs to her cell with Chae, her celly." Mystro asked.

Logan looked up toward the ceiling in deep thought before she spoke. "Well, Chae ain't bad."

"Yep, she's my right hand in the kitchen, y'all be cool in there together!" Mystro said excitedly.

"Aight, that works for me, but you still should have told me straight up." Logan reiterated.

"You right, that's on me." Mystro felt bad. "I'ma-"

"Logan, leave us alone for a minute." C.O. Michael said as he walked into their cell.

"Oh, nah it's cool if she stays C.O., she knows what's going on and we actually-"

"Step out, inmate Logan." C.O. Michael said cutting Mystro off. He was stern and without kindness.

Logan cut her eyes at Mystro before she jumped up and hurried out the cell.

Mystro looked up at C.O. Michael confused but waited for him to speak.

He walked in and up to Mystro. "I was doing you a favor, why did you involve Logan?" He asked.

Mystro took one step back. "Uh–."

"Answer me!"

He was cold and it put her on pause and she was reminded once again that he was police.

"You know how shit gets around in here. I didn't have to tell her nothing she already knew about the move. And instead of her going in there with-"

"Well, it don't matter no way. Nobody's moving." He stated.

"Huh?" Mystro asked, confused.

"I got the ok on the cell change but when I went to get Dent, she didn't wanna come." C.O. Michael explained, as if he were angry.

"I don't get it. Why you ain't make her move?" Mystro asked.

"Make her move? I couldn't do that. This was a request not a prison order. We can't intervene like that." C.O. Michael advised.

Mystro sat down on her bunk and put her head into her hands.

"What about something like on the basis of it being a danger to her well-being or

BY C. WASH

health? Could you intervene then?" Mystro asked desperately.

"Yeah, but Dent would have to make that request herself and from what I can see, she's not interested in doing that." C.O. Michael explained.

"What is wrong with her, man?" Mystro blurted out loud.

"Look, I'm not sure, and to be honest I don't give a fuck. But keep me out of your games and your requests! Are we clear?" He stared down into her eyes intensely.

"I only asked because you said–."

"Are we clear, inmate!" He reiterated.

She nodded and he walked away.

"Inmate?" She repeated to herself.

It was the first time he addressed her in that way, but she would never forget.

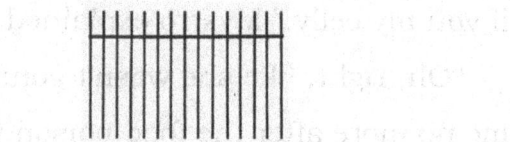

Mystro walked into Baby Dom and Bruiser's cell. Baby Dom was lying on her bunk with her face towards the wall.

She had on a white tank top that displayed red marks on her left shoulder. Her locs were pulled back and held together with a black and red cotton hair tie.

"Baby Dom," Mystro called out.

Baby Dom didn't move.

"Baby Dom," she called out again.

Baby Dom didn't budge.

"I know you can hear me. Why you ain't come with C.O. Michael to move into my cell?" Mystro asked as she walked up closer to her bunk.

Baby Dom sighed.

"I want you out of this bitch! Bruiser only fucking with you like she is because she feel like she can. She won't be able to bother you if you my celly." Mystro explained.

"Oh, right, like she wasn't gonna fuck with me no more after the food poison thing too huh?" Baby Dom asked sarcastically.

**BY C. WASH**

Mystro sucked her teeth. "Aight, BD, I underestimated this crazy bitch. But that's why I'm trying to get you moved." She admitted.

Baby Dom turned her body around slowly to face Mystro.

Mystro rolled her eyes when she saw her bruised and strained face. Shit was getting worse.

It wasn't just the bruises that had her on edge, but the daunt and distant look in Baby Dom's eyes.

She felt like crying.

"Look at your fucking face, man! Why you wanna keep putting up with this bamma when you don't have to?" Mystro yelled as her voice cracked.

"You want the truth, fam?" Baby Dom asked.

"Yes, please." Mystro pleaded, nodding her head.

"Cuz I'm afraid." Baby Dom admitted while looking down.

"Afraid of what? I just told you she not gonna be able to touch you once you move out. I got you." Mystro ran up closer to the bunk. "I promise."

She had to step on Bruiser's bed so she could be face to face with Baby Dom, but she didn't care because, fuck Bruiser.

"I told you I got your back! You my nigga and I'ma make-"

Baby Dom shook her head and closed her eyes. "I ain't scared for me." Baby Dom admitted.

Mystro looked at her confused. "Then who?"

"I'm afraid for you."

It was over, Mystro could no longer hold her tears.

"Baby Dom, come here, man!" Mystro demanded as she stepped down and backed up to give her room.

Baby Dom slowly climbed down off her bunk to face Mystro.

"When we first met you, all I saw was this young, short, wild and crazy dom lady and I thought you was a straight up lunch box." She recalled.

Baby Dom smirked.

"But the more and more you wouldn't leave us alone, I realized I liked having you around." Mystro confessed. "You like my 'lil brother, fam. It took me a while to get my shit together, but I promise, I'm in this with you now." She looked down into Baby Dom's eyes.

Baby Dom looked up at Mystro and a tear rolled down her cheek.

"I gotta plan." She put her hand on Baby Dom's shoulder gently. "Just keep your head down, and move with that same energy like we beefing still, but know that I will get you out of this shit with Bruiser and we gonna be cool, together. You got my word!" Mystro stared at her intensely.

HERSBAND MATERIAL 2: JAILHOUSE BUTCH

Baby Dom nodded and looked up at Mystro and for the first time since she'd been in prison, Mystro saw hope in her eyes.

**BY C. WASH**

# CHAPTER TWENTY-ONE
## MYSTRO

After getting carried by her girl for the fiftieth time in a row, Bruiser decided to let off steam in the rec room on the basketball court.

She was just about to get her blood going with her comrade but when she tossed the ball in her direction, Mystro trotted in and grabbed it instead.

"Fuck is you doing?" Bruiser asked, turning up her nose like she smelled something foul.

With the ball in one hand and the other raised, Mystro said, "So what, you can't handle a little one on one?"

"Oh, please stop playing with my life! This ain't no stove, you can't fuck with me on this court! I'll stomp you into this pine." Bruiser boasted.

"Oh, yeah? Well, let's see, check." Mystro bounced the ball towards Bruiser's direction.

Bruiser caught the bounced pass.

"So what we playing to?" Bruiser asked Mystro seriously.

"Five, by ones." Mystro replied.

"What's the stakes? I mean what do I get when I win all this shit?" Bruiser asked sarcastically.

"If *I* win you leave me and Baby Dom alone completely."

Bruiser sucked her teeth. "And when *I* win, what I get?" She asked again.

"You just leave her alone." Mystro replied.

"Fuck is up with you and shawty?" She frowned.

Mystro ignored her inquiry. "You in or not?"

"I asked you a fucking question?" Bruiser insisted. "She eating your box or something?"

Mystro was heated. "At the end of the day, you got flunkies already." Mystro cut her eyes towards Cinnamon.

**BY C. WASH**

"Yeah, well I want another one." Bruiser smirked and dribbled the ball between her legs.

"Like I said, you got flunkies, she done being one of 'em." Mystro informed.

"She gonna keep being whatever the fuck I want her to be." Bruiser replied. Her nostrils flared.

Mystro stepped closer.

Bruiser did the same.

At that moment Mystro could hear Native in her ear. Blaming her for the state of her circumstances.

She knew she had two options. She could knock Bruiser the fuck out and they could keep going back and forth with Baby Dom caught in the middle or she could try one last time to appeal to her softer side.

If this bitch had one.

Mystro decided to bite her tongue.

"I know her from back in the day."

Bruiser smiled.

She liked where this was going. "I know."

"Well if you know, then you understand why I don't want her fucked with. So, are we gonna settle this like two respectable niggas from DC? Or are we gonna let this prison shit take over?" Mystro asked, ready for whatever Bruiser decided.

Bruiser contemplated her options. Although she'd never seen Mystro play, she knew she herself was good with the rock. However, given the seriousness of the stakes she had a feeling she may not come out on the winning end right now.

On the other hand, she was very competitive, especially where she knew she could shine. So she chest passed the ball to Mystro hard and said, "let's go."

But before the game ensued, Mystro wanted clarification.

"Aight, so if I win, *all* is dead. And if you win, you choose." She confirmed and passed the ball back.

Bruiser smiled.

"Yep, check." She bounced passed the ball toward Mystro.

Mystro received the ball and yelled, "Check." She bounced the ball back.

Bruiser dribbled the ball toward the right and pulled up for a jump shot.

It went in.

"One nothing." Bruiser shouted, with a grin across her face.

Mystro grabbed the rebound and bounced it back toward Bruiser.

"Bruiser didn't check the ball again, instead she drove the lane and elbowed Mystro before she laid it up and into the basket.

"Two nothing." Bruiser chuckled.

Cinnamon looked on with a smile in the background. At that moment her boss was getting the best of Mystro.

Mystro took a deep breath and locked in.

"You not gonna get a shot, Northeast, you might as well let me hit this three and call it game." Bruiser laughed.

Mystro said nothing. She rolled her scrub pants leg up and got into a defensive stance.

"Check," Bruiser yelled.

Mystro passed her the ball.

Bruiser pump faked, then went up to shoot.

Mystro blocked her shot and grabbed the ball.

She dribbled to the top of the key. Then drove the lane for a quick layup.

Cinnamon yelled out, "One to two."

Bruiser shot her the death glare.

Cinnamon covered her mouth and closed her eyes.

Mystro bounced the ball to Bruiser, and she reluctantly returned it.

"Kobe!" Mystro yelled as she pulled up for a jump shot.

It went in.

After she checked the ball, Mystro dribbled and pulled up for a ten-foot jump shot off the backboard.

Bruiser was visibly heated.

Mystro got the ball back and drove the lane for a left-hand layup. And just like that, she was well in the lead.

"Four two." Mystro reminded Bruiser.

Bruiser stared at her with disdain. She couldn't guard her.

Mystro dribbled the ball and yelled, "Point."

She passed the ball to Bruiser to check it, but it bounced off Bruiser's chest and rolled back toward Mystro.

Bruiser smacked the ground and got into a deep defensive stance to try and guard Mystro tight.

Mystro bounced passed the ball to herself through Bruiser's legs then pulled up for the game winning jump shot.

It went in.

"Game." Mystro said.

Bruiser stood in disbelief and anger.

Cinnamon dropped her head down and threw her hands up in disappointment.

Bruiser wiped down her face with her hand and let out a deep breath.

"So, we good right?" Mystro asked for confirmation while she palmed the ball in one hand.

Bruiser, with a scowl on her face, smirked and said, "Yep, we good. All is dead."

BY C. WASH

# CHAPTER TWENTY-TWO

# MYSTRO

**M**ystro replayed the game with Bruiser over again in her mind. If she could admit it to herself, it was some of her best work. Just the look on Bruiser's face was enough to make her smile.

In her opinion, this was what she needed to save Baby Dom and make the best of her remaining time. She couldn't wait to get with Native who in her mind had been too opinionated.

But for the moment, Mystro won, and she was grateful.

Lying on her bed face up, she heard a loud scream. She sat up on the edge and frowned then looked at her open door.

A wave of people moving from the left to the right, struck her.

"Fuck is going on?" She said to herself.

Feet planted on the floor, slowly she walked to the door. For some reason at that moment, she felt as if warm hands were holding her back. Preventing her from stepping out.

But curiosity got the best of her.

Pushing out of the entryway, she took her position amongst the crowd. At first it was hard to see the object of everyone's attention. But soon it became obvious.

Bruiser's cell?

Nah.

Baby Dom's cell?

It was one in the same, but the first way sounded easier. Less painful. Shoving past people who all of a sudden seemed to be in her way, she moved toward the attraction.

Elbow pointed and stabbing in people's sides.

Fist pushes toward their backs.

Whatever was necessary, she did, until she happened upon the door. Yep, it was Bruiser's cell.

Nah.

**222**

Baby Dom's cell.

The pain she had in her stomach before even seeing what was happening felt final. Like if she didn't see her friend's face, life as she knew it would be over. It wasn't until that moment that she realized how much she truly cared for the young bull.

Of course she fucked with her.

After all, she made a sworn pact with her enemy for her safety.

But this was different.

It wasn't until that moment that she truly realized Baby Dom wasn't just Baby Dom. She was the little homie.

She was family.

Shoving a little more, she saw what she wished she hadn't.

The bottom of Baby Dom's body was on her bed, but the top part was hanging off. Her eyes open.

Life gone.

Mystro knocked niggas to the left and right to move closer. Inmates moaned but now was not the time to try her. They knew it so they moved out her way.

It wasn't until she was inside fully that she saw Bruiser in the corner smiling.

"Junkie must've shot herself up with a bad batch," Bruiser said, announcing her innocence without being direct. "I'm not surprised. Are y'all?"

Most mumbled no.

Mystro trembled.

Slowly Bruiser approached and placed a heavy hand on Mystro's shoulder. With her lips close to her ear, so that she could feel her hot, funky breath, she said, "I win. Always."

And walked out.

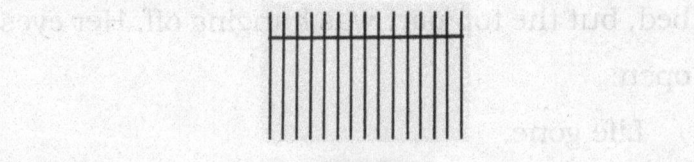

**NATIVE**

**BY C. WASH**

Native decided it was best to stop the war with her girl. It wasn't that serious in the first place. But more than it all, it was a waste of time.

So when she stepped through the door the only thing she said was, "Put your shit on. I'ma take you to get a bite to eat."

That was all Brisa needed to bounce around the walls of their apartment like a trapped gnat.

Native on the other hand decided to grab a shower.

So she wasn't there.

But Brisa was when the call came through. "Hello!"

*"You have a collect call from, Mystro, an inmate at Washington Alley Prison For Women. To Accept--."*

CLICK.

There was no fucking way she was about to have her night destroyed. Not for Mystro's inmate, prison, dyke chronicles.

Nah, she was spending the night with her baby.

And at the same time, pausing, momentarily, the worst news Native would receive in years.

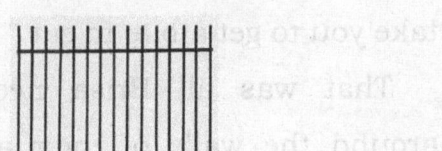

Brisa got on Native's nerves all fucking evening.

But this time, she truly didn't get what was going wrong.

When she told her to get dressed to hang out, she was sincerely trying to make a go at the relationship or whatever. Afterall, she didn't have a problem putting Mystro in her place.

She figured it was time to take her own advice.

The only thing was, Brisa spent the first part of the night, worrying about the broad on the left with the big titties and the red hair. And the other part of the night, worrying about a cook, who only passed their table to go in the back for work.

"I know what you doing." Brisa said, her upper lip over the rim of a glass of Hennessy that Native didn't want her to have in the first place. Because when she had too much, it made her breath smell like shit.

This was supposed to be classy.

"What you talking about?" Native asked reluctantly, looking over at Brisa with disgust.

"You been staring at that bitch's titties all night." Brisa stated.

"What?" Native turned up her nose like the air stunk.

"If you were gonna just come out here and treat me like shit, why even invite me out?" Brisa asked sincerely.

Native wanted to dip and leave Brisa and her brown liquor to the hood shit by which she was accustomed.

But she was growing and had to be better, right?

"Listen, bae, all I wanna do is spend time with--."

"And what about that bitch who walked past the table? Who was trying to--."

"Fuck is going on?" Native asked. "For real? 'Cuz I've known you long enough. What you guilty about this time?"

Brisa paused for a moment. How the fuck Native get onto her so quickly? In the back of Brisa's mind it was best to start an argument now because she was certain when that call came back, that Native would be heated.

Lips back over the rim of the Hennessey glass Brisa said, "Nothing."

Native didn't get an answer to what was troubling her until later on that night.

The moment Native stepped in the house after *Failed Date Night;* the phone rang. To get away from Henny Lips, she rushed to pick it up without even looking at the caller ID screen.

"Who is--."

*"You have a collect call from, "Pick up Na-,"*
*an inmate at..."*

Native didn't need the rest. She followed the instructions. Accepted the call. And learned what she didn't even know was possible.

"Fuck you been?" Mystro yelled, her voice filled with anger and pain.

"What you--."

"I been calling you all fucking day! I did what you said. Tried to handle shit right! And she killed the lil homie! She fucking killed her!"

Mystro continued to pour out her heart not caring who may be listening in on the call.

Native was present but her heart was hardened.

"She...she gone?"

"This shit hit hard, Nae! It hit hard. I...I can't fuckin..." Mystro's words were fragmented like text messages, but she got the jist.

**HERSBAND MATERIAL 2: JAILHOUSE BUTCH**

A family member, someone they both loved, was dead.

And then Native's eyes rolled onto the bitch in the corner. Who was supposed to be her girl. She rejected the call.

The look in Native's eyes told Brisa everything she needed to know.

First, that their relationship would never be the same.

And second, that her friend needed her now more than ever.

"Mystro, I got you. I promise."

**BY C. WASH**

# CHAPTER TWENTY-THREE

# MYSTRO

**M**ystro was in the private visitor's hall with her lawyer. He came to advise her that he found a solid loophole in her case and if it worked, she'd be released in a matter of days.

This was great news!

But you wouldn't know it if you looked into the room. Mystro, who was visibly distraught, could not hear what her lawyer tried to explain.

Her face was puffy, eyes were bloodshot red, and she sat slumped so far down in her chair that she was almost under the table.

She could not believe that less than twenty-four hours ago, her homie was killed.

She was hurt and pissed at the same time.

As her lawyer continued to explain the technicalities of her case and possible release, Mystro glanced down at her wrist.

During the commotion when she found Baby Dom, she felt like she had an outer body experience. She vaguely remembered being in the cell looking at her lifeless friend and pondering what went wrong.

"Mystro, did you hear what I said? You can be out of here in a matter of days. Aren't you excited?" Her lawyer asked.

Mystro looked up at him blankly and without any words, got up and walked toward the door.

"C.O.," she yelled. "I'm ready." She called out to leave.

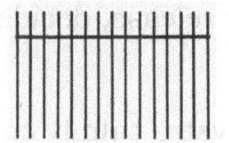

When someone died in prison, there was an unwritten rule that the people closest to the deceased have respect paid to them.

It could be favors being done for them or gifts given to them.

This was the case for Mystro. All day long inmates stopped past her cell and dropped off snacks, soap, books, drawings, homemade cards and more to pay homage to her lost friend.

Mystro accepted the gifts out of respect but wanted none of them. She was lost and furious.

She was tired of sitting idly waiting to see if the prison would formally charge Bruiser in Baby Dom's death.

Mystro had enough and, although any moves she was thinking about making could jeopardize her release, decided to institute prison justice.

"Logan," Mystro calmly called out.

"What's up, sugar?" Logan replied.

She paused briefly before she spoke.

"I know you can get anything in here, but can you *really* get your hands on anything?" Mystro asked as she stood up and looked her cellmate in her eyes.

Logan returned her stare and replied, "Absolutely. Anything you need. Just say the word."

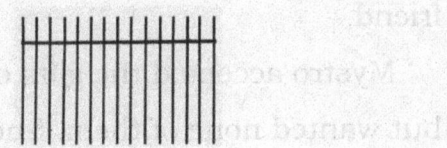

Bruiser was in the shower, laughing and joking with Cinnamon and two of her other flunkies.

"She thought I was gonna be sised that she wanted back on my visits," Bruiser bragged. "I was like nah, *I'm good, slut.*"

BY C. WASH

"You ain't do that shit," Cinnamon said as she took a soapy washcloth to her hairy pussy.

"I'm telling you what the fuck happened, young," Bruiser continued, slamming the wet cloth over her pits. "I was sick of her being a whore. Anyway, I put her friend on my visits now. She on it hard too! Can't stop coming down." She smiled.

Cinnamon and the gang placed fists to the mouth in happiness.

"Damn, you fucking her friend now?" Flunky Two asked.

"I said what I said. It's--."

Suddenly, all jokes stopped.

With the same speediness as a person holding a remote and pressing mute, when Mystro walked inside.

She didn't say a word.

Didn't need to, to be honest.

Her gaze was directly on Bruiser.

For a second, nothing but water from the shower and Cinnamon doing her leveled best to get the soap out of her pussy could be heard.

And then, "Fuck you want, freak?" Bruiser asked, trying to gain control.

Silence.

"Why you staring at me and shit?" Bruiser continued.

Silence.

When Cinnamon was soap free, she turned the water off and grabbed her towel, wrapping it around her body tightly. Bare feet slapping the ground in Mystro's direction, she meant to earn her stripes by punching Mystro in the mouth.

Instead, she was dropped to the floor.

Mystro hit her so quickly, most didn't see it happen. But Cinnamon did when her brain shifted in her skull as she hit the ground.

This was about Bruiser.

If anybody else wanted a ticket, Mystro was perfectly willing to show them to their seats. But it was best to stay out the way.

Turning off the water, Bruiser dried off. Covering her lower half.

Mystro stepped closer.

"I told you to leave her alone." Her nostrils flared and forehead vein popped. "You couldn't do it though. Why?"

"You still crying about that bitch? Because now I'm sure she definitely ate that box."

They all laughed but not with the same vigor. Besides, Cinnamon was barely conscious and the others were rightfully scared. When someone was in the mood to commit murder, it was written all over their bodies.

So at that moment, Mystro was a newspaper.

"I told you to leave her alone and you lost the game. Straight up! But why didn't you?" Mystro asked with pain in her inquiry. In her heart it wasn't about Bruiser's testimony. She knew the answer would fuel her rage.

And she needed the anger for her next moves.

Bruiser wasn't going to waste her time, so she said, "Man, get this bitch up out my face."

Cinnamon peeled herself off the floor while she and the other two charged Mystro.

But shit hit differently.

Literally.

Mystro held back her rage up until this moment. And if they wanted to be the appetizer for the murder she intended to commit, then so be it.

One by one, Cinnamon was the first to step up. She swung a wild left, but it didn't land, hitting nothing but air. Then, still dizzy from the last blow, she slipped and fell.

Unable to regain her bearings, her chin hit the floor.

Mystro stomped the back of her head, and now she was definitely out cold.

Then there was the Flunky Two, who was jive scared. She yelled, "Ahhhgghhhhhh!" As she ran after Mystro in an attempt to get out on her with crazy arms.

Mystro dodged her barrage of wild fists swings and dropped another one with a blow to the temple. She, also, was out cold.

At this point Mystro didn't understand why Bruiser sent either of them her way.

It was obvious they couldn't wreck.

But Flunky Three appeared ready.

She swung a left and then a right. Both landed on Mystro's face. They put her off guard too because as she tried to regain her footing, she realized it was easier said than done.

Mystro was stunned.

Seeing stars.

Where did number three come from anyway?

It was at that moment that she realized that it was about to be a war and so that's exactly what happened.

Blow after blow landed until Mystro felt the earth weaken beneath her feet. If she continued to get hit in the way she had, she would not survive and get at Bruiser.

And so, she pulled out the shank that Logan was able to secure from her bra and made an attempt to stab her by wielding it wildly.

Flunky Three's eyes widened in fear.

But Flunky Three, thinking on her feet, knocked the knife from her hand, and stole her in the face once more.

However, Mystro, although exhausted, moved quickly to pick it up and stabbed her in the right side and then the left.

Now it was Mystro who got the best of her. It was Mystro who was in control. Flunky Three was on the floor, writhing in pain. Afraid of death that she was sure would come.

240

With the blood draining from Flunky Three's body, the room was stuffy and hot.

Only the sounds of dripping water could be heard. The other sound was deep breathing and an elevated heartbeat.

Everything happened so fast.

But if she could go back and do it over again what would be different?

As she stood there trying to get a solid rhythm in her breath, in her heart, she contemplated what was her next step.

Standing over the body she needed a plan and she needed one now.

If she ran, there was no guarantee someone wouldn't see her. In her condition she was sure they wouldn't understand. But if she stayed, how would she get out of this?

She needed a miracle.

While realizing that she was undeserving.

"What the fuck am I gonna do now?" She said out loud to herself.

HERSBAND MATERIAL 2: JAILHOUSE BUTCH

The only thing she could think to do at the moment, pray.

"God, you know my heart. You know I didn't mean for things to go this way. If you see fit to get me out of this predicament, I will never be put in it again. Amen."

"Is this bitch over here praying?" Bruiser yelled out. "Asking God for help? Don't you know? God don't visit this prison."

It wasn't until that moment that Mystro remembered she wasn't alone. After all, how could Bruiser stand ringside and not help her friends?

Slowly Mystro looked over at her.

While Bruiser took advantage of Mystro's disorientation and the fact that she was winded after fighting three people and possibly killing one of them.

Knocking Mystro to the floor where Cinnamon, Flunky Two and Flunky Three lay, Bruiser got on top of her body.

It's like she watched everything Mystro did in the battle. Because the first blow struck Mystro on the side of the temple.

The next shook her left jaw.

Bruiser looked maniacal as she struck her in all exposed parts of her body. For a second, Mystro gave up. After all, she killed another person, Baby Dom was dead, and it was her fault.

Why live?

Why fight back?

Perhaps this was karma coming for its due.

And then she saw Baby Dom's face in her mind. It was during a time when they were out in the world.

Mystro was sitting on the porch of Margaret's house with Native on her right. They were talking about life, and dreams, and things that seemed so trivial at the time.

With the sun beaming behind her, Baby Dom bopped down the block with a smile on her face. She always brought life to any space she inhabited.

*"Whatever y'all gonna do, take me with you,"* was all she said that day.

*"You don't even know where we going!"* Mystro yelled out.

*"It don't matter! I'm rolling."*

They laughed.

For some reason, that statement was enough for Mystro to remember that when she saw Baby Dom's lifeless body, she took two things from the cell without Bruiser knowing.

One was the picture of she, Native and Baby Dom.

And the second, was her hair tie.

No, scratch that.

It could actually be considered a shoestring. It had the same length and width. To be honest she had no business having it in prison but Baby Dom loved the way it tamed her locs on the street so snuck it inside.

The thing was, no one seemed to notice.

**BY C. WASH**

No one seemed to care about Baby Dom in there but Mystro.

From the day she saw Baby Dom's lifeless body until that moment, Mystro had worn it on her wrist, but it was this that she would use in the moment.

With all the power she had left, Mystro raised her head and bit down into Bruiser's left titty.

Hard.

So hard that she bit off the nipple before spitting it out.

Bruiser screamed out in pain.

Mystro used this moment to wiggle from up under her body. Sliding toward Bruiser who was gripping her chest, she eased behind her, wrapped her legs tightly over her belly and used the hair tie to wrap around her neck.

Bruiser fought with all her might.

Fingernails clawing at the sides of Mystro's face.

None of that shit mattered.

She pulled, squeezed and tugged.

*"Whatever y'all gonna do, take me with you,"* Baby Dom's voice rang in her head again.

Mystro pulled the string harder.

*"Whatever y'all gonna do, take me with you..."*

Pull.

Harder.

Baby Dom's voice continued to play in her head, until Bruiser wasn't fighting anymore.

She wasn't moving anymore.

She wasn't breathing anymore.

And C.O. Michael was standing in the doorway.

Mystro rolled on her side and let out the first real cry since Baby Dom was killed. She would take her with her for the rest of her life. She knew it with all her heart.

Even if life meant being in prison.

Observing the bloody scene, C.O. Michael walked up to her. Gripped her by the shirt and said, "Listen to me, stop fucking crying."

246

She tried but it was hard.

"Stop fucking crying now." Spit flew from his mouth and mixed with the tears on her face.

Mystro realized at that moment who was talking to her and calmed down.

"Rinse your face in that shower in two seconds and then put on that shirt over there. After that, get the fuck out. I won't say it again. This is your last chance."

Mystro didn't know what was happening. She blinked several times to regain her composure.

She was having another outer body experience, but she got up and did all he said. Rinsed her face in the shower and put on Bruiser's shirt.

Looking at him once more, she walked briskly out the door.

# CHAPTER TWENTY-FOUR
## MYSTRO

Not to be corny but the sun was shining, and the birds were singing when Mystro walked out of the final door from the prison where she'd spent over a year of her life.

Although not a lot of time had passed, she felt like she was way older and experienced a lot.

When she hit the parking lot, she was relieved when she saw her best friend, Native standing outside of her car waiting.

Native's face was scrunched up until she saw her homie and then a look of calm took over.

Mystro walked up to Native and the two embraced in a long and intense hug.

When Mystro tried to pull away, Native held on a bit longer.

When the two finally separated, Native's face was covered in tears as the realization of Baby Dom being gone struck her deeper.

"She gone, Nae, but I made it right." Mystro said with intensity as she stared at Native.

Native looked up at Mystro confused at first, but when she saw her eyes, she knew exactly what she meant.

"I need to say something to you." Native started.

Mystro took a deep breath as she prepared to hear the worst.

"This shit ain't just on you, it's on me too." Native confessed.

Mystro started to tear up again.

"We didn't do all we could to look out for the homie, but we did what we knew how to do. She's not physically here no more but will always ride with us." Native explained.

Mystro wiped her tears and nodded.

"Our job is to never look back, and always keep her memory alive."

Mystro agreed and the two embraced once again.

"Come on, let's get the fuck out of here before they make us both go back."

Mystro smirked, "Never again."

"Speaking of never again, I'm done with Brisa." Native said pulling her black skull cap down over her braids and opening the car door.

Mystro lifted her chin up high. Her mouth dropped open, and her eyebrows rose.

"What the fuck happened, son?" She asked in shock.

Native shook her head. "Man, shawty was on some whole other shit, you knew that, but what did it for me was trying to come between us. I was done and packed my shit after I talked to you that night." Native admitted with sorrow in her eyes.

Mystro put her hand on her shoulder. "I'm sorry, fam."

"It's cool. I am what I am and some lady's girlfriend ain't it." Native continued.

Mystro nodded her head and smiled and without looking back they got into the car and Native drove off.

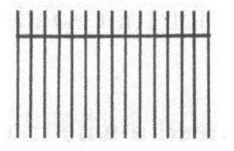

## TWO WEEKS LATER

Mystro walked into her new apartment.

It wasn't in the best neighborhood or the flyest spot, but with Native's help, she was able to get a place after she was released, and it seemed surreal.

There was nothing in there but a made-up pallet on the floor. Which at the moment and considering where she just came from, was more than all she needed.

It felt like heaven.

She threw her keys down by the door and layed down on her makeshift bed.

Mystro always sought after what she didn't have, a stable life that included a family. She had her dad for the most part growing up, but without her mom, she was always looking for that solid foundation, or so she thought.

She didn't need a wife to complete her.

She had Native, her mom, Margaret and she used to have Baby Dom. It didn't appear how she thought it would but that was her family.

She didn't know what she would do next but for the first time in her life, she felt at peace.

BY C. WASH

# EPILOGUE

**N**ative planned a huge welcome home party for Mystro.

The party was to take place at Margaret's house, Native's mother's where the two spent many years living together.

Mystro was on her way out the door to try and enjoy herself for the first time in a long time.

"Son, make sure you bring your slow ass on." Native yelled at Mystro through the phone. Clearly, she had gotten the party started on her own. She sounded like she was about three shots deep.

"Already in route, save me some liquor nigga." Mystro teased.

As she hung up from the call, she locked her door and made her way down the hallway steps and out to the parking lot where her Uber driver awaited.

When she got outside, she didn't see her ride waiting although he said he was there.

"What the fuck?"

As she peered around the corner, she saw a face she was not expecting or prepared to see.

C.O. Michael stepped out of a vehicle and walked toward her with purpose.

Mystro stood motionless.

"Mystro Mason, what up? Why you look scared, you ain't happy to see me?" He asked with outstretched arms and a huge smile plastered on his face.

Mystro was completely confused on what to say.

"I know you may be at a loss for words but let me help you out." He started.

"Wh...what are you doing here?" Mystro found her voice and asked.

"Well to put you at ease, you good. I'm not here to drag you back to prison. Unless--" he paused and smiled rubbing his goatee.

"Unless what?" Mystro blurted out.

"Well...I came to collect." C.O. Michael replied.

"Collect?" Mystro questioned. "Collect, what?"

"You." He flatly stated and smirked.

Mystro felt like the ground under her feet was moving. She opened her mouth to speak, but nothing came out.

"Oh, you thought that get out of jail shit was free?" Michael asked. "Nah, I put in work for you. I set your little fight club scene up to make it look as though Cinnamon took out Patterson, Jenkins and Drew."

"I'm still lost. I-I don't understand. Like where is all this coming from?" Mystro asked, confused.

"I don't know why you don't understand. I was never too far from you. Play the tapes back, didn't you ever wonder why I always found my way to you when trouble was arising?" Michael replied as he walked closer towards Mystro. "When you were in the rec

255

HERSBAND MATERIAL 2: JAILHOUSE BUTCH

with Patterson and Cinnamon and y'all almost fought. I came in at the right moment because I saw tensions were flaring." He smiled.

Mystro felt sick.

"Or the time when Patterson had you snatched and was about to jump you. I rolled around to the side entrance and watched just in case I needed to bust in there but to my surprise, I saw my baby could hold her own." He boasted as if Mystro belonged to him.

Mystro put her hand on her forehead to ease her thumping headache.

"Not to mention the last time. I knew I couldn't come right in because I wanted to see if you could finally take care of that bitch." He continued. "I gotta admit, it was a little scary when she rushed you at the end, but once again you came out on top."

Mystro grabbed the sides of her head.

"Don't even get me started on all the prison garbage I had to eat and fake love to win you over." He laughed. "Don't get me wrong, you a good cook. But the ingredients in there were trash."

"But why? I mean like why were you doing all that?" She tried to control her breath.

"I told you. I did it for *You*." Michael said seriously. "I've never met a woman like you in my life, Mystro. You're fun, easy on the eyes, you love football and not to mention you can cook! You're perfect for me."

Mystro ran her hands backwards through her hair. Her eyes bulged out of her head. Was this real?

"Um, C.O, I-,"

"Just Mike, I'm not your C.O. no more." Michael advised with a smile.

"O-Ok Mike, um, I'm flattered, but I'm gay. I like women." Mystro explained. She swallowed the lump in her throat unsure of how he would receive her news.

"Oh, yeah, I know. That's cool, I like 'em too. That's no big deal, I mean I know I'm a man, but I'll grow on you." He winked.

Mystro felt faint.

"So, look, I sent your little Uber driver away. But don't fret, I'ma escort you around town." He assured her. "I'ma escort you around your life. We can keep what we do private. From the women you deal with and my wife."

Mystro's breathing was rapid, and her heartbeat felt like it was coming through her ears.

"I hear your homie throwing you a party. I can't wait to officially meet her. Based on y'alls emails, I know how close you two are." He replied.

Mystro was terrified. What was she gonna do? She felt like she wanted to break out running, but where would she go?

"Well, since we're all caught up it's no point in standing around out here. You ready to bounce? Because I don't know about you, but I need a drink."

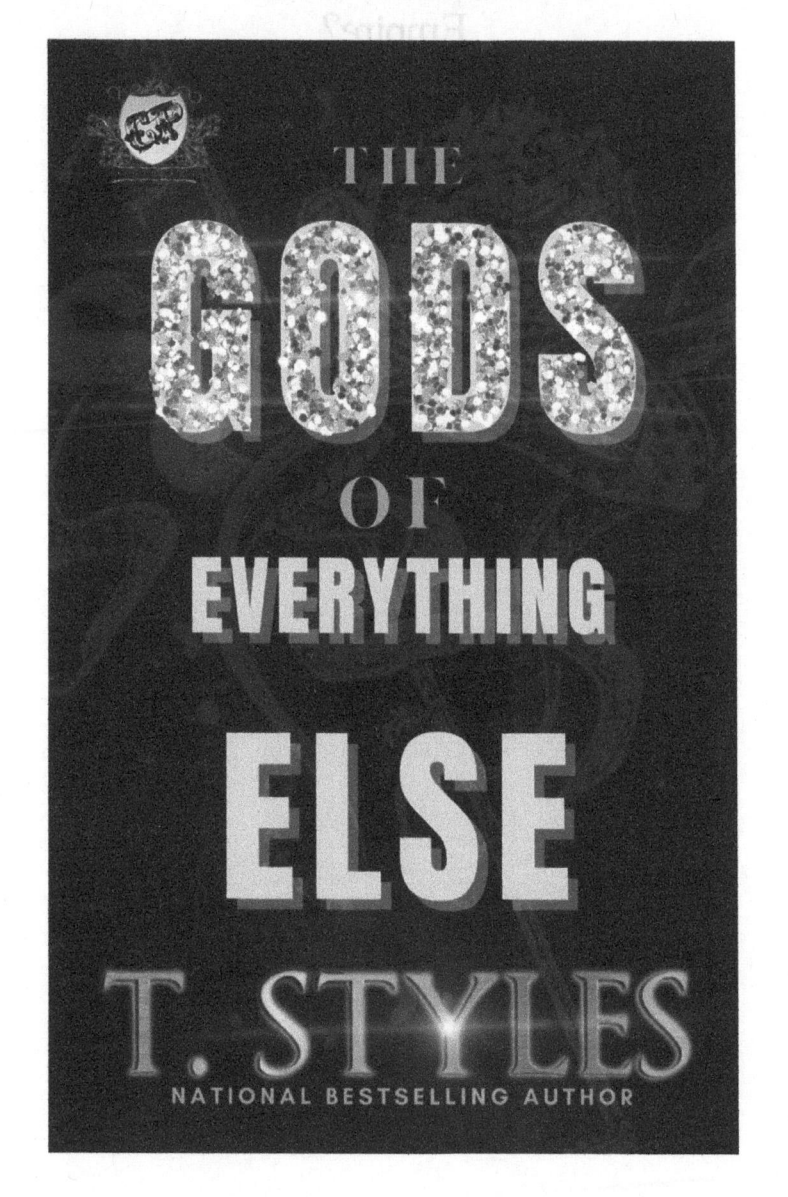

THE

GODS

OF

EVERYTHING

ELSE

T. STYLES

NATIONAL BESTSELLING AUTHOR

HERSBAND MATERIAL 2: JAILHOUSE BUTCH

Are you looking to build your Book Empire?

Do you Need Help?

Visit:
www.theelitewritersacademy.com

For Planners, Courses and Templates

HERSBAND MATERIAL 2: JAILHOUSE BUTCH

CARTEL PUBLICATIONS

PRESENTS

# The Cartel Publications Order Form

www.thecartelpublications.com

Inmates **ONLY** receive novels for $12.00 per book **PLUS** shipping fee **PER BOOK.**

(Mail Order **MUST** come from inmate directly to receive discount)

| | | |
|---|---|---|
| Shyt List 1 | _____ | $15.00 |
| Shyt List 2 | _____ | $15.00 |
| Shyt List 3 | _____ | $15.00 |
| Shyt List 4 | _____ | $15.00 |
| Shyt List 5 | _____ | $15.00 |
| Shyt List 6 | _____ | $15.00 |
| Pitbulls In A Skirt | _____ | $15.00 |
| Pitbulls In A Skirt 2 | _____ | $15.00 |
| Pitbulls In A Skirt 3 | _____ | $15.00 |
| Pitbulls In A Skirt 4 | _____ | $15.00 |
| Pitbulls In A Skirt 5 | _____ | $15.00 |
| Victoria's Secret | _____ | $15.00 |
| Poison 1 | _____ | $15.00 |
| Poison 2 | _____ | $15.00 |
| Hell Razor Honeys | _____ | $15.00 |
| Hell Razor Honeys 2 | _____ | $15.00 |
| A Hustler's Son | _____ | $15.00 |
| A Hustler's Son 2 | _____ | $15.00 |
| Black and Ugly | _____ | $15.00 |
| Black and Ugly As Ever | _____ | $15.00 |
| Ms Wayne & The Queens of DC **(LGBT)** | _____ | $15.00 |
| Black And The Ugliest | _____ | $15.00 |
| Year Of The Crackmom | _____ | $15.00 |
| Deadheads | _____ | $15.00 |
| The Face That Launched A Thousand Bullets | _____ | $15.00 |
| The Unusual Suspects | _____ | $15.00 |
| Paid In Blood | _____ | $15.00 |
| Raunchy | _____ | $15.00 |
| Raunchy 2 | _____ | $15.00 |
| Raunchy 3 | _____ | $15.00 |
| Mad Maxxx (4th Book Raunchy Series) | _____ | $15.00 |
| Quita's Dayscare Center | _____ | $15.00 |
| Quita's Dayscare Center 2 | _____ | $15.00 |
| Pretty Kings | _____ | $15.00 |

**BY C. WASH**

| | | |
|---|---|---|
| Pretty Kings 2 | _____ | $15.00 |
| Pretty Kings 3 | _____ | $15.00 |
| Pretty Kings 4 | _____ | $15.00 |
| Silence Of The Nine | _____ | $15.00 |
| Silence Of The Nine 2 | _____ | $15.00 |
| Silence Of The Nine 3 | _____ | $15.00 |
| | | |
| Prison Throne | _____ | $15.00 |
| Drunk & Hot Girls | _____ | $15.00 |
| Hersband Material **(LGBT)** _ _____ | | $15.00 |
| The End: How To Write A _____ | | $15.00 |
| Bestselling Novel In 30 Days (Non-Fiction Guide) | | |
| Upscale Kittens | _____ | $15.00 |
| Wake & Bake Boys | _____ | $15.00 |
| Young & Dumb | _____ | $15.00 |
| Young & Dumb 2: Vyce's Getback _____ | | $15.00 |
| Tranny 911 **(LGBT)** | _____ | $15.00 |
| Tranny 911: Dixie's Rise **(LGBT)** _____ | | $15.00 |
| First Comes Love, Then Comes Murder _____ | | $15.00 |
| Luxury Tax | _____ | $15.00 |
| The Lying King | _____ | $15.00 |
| Crazy Kind Of Love | _____ | $15.00 |
| Goon | _____ | $15.00 |
| And They Call Me God | _____ | $15.00 |
| The Ungrateful Bastards | _____ | $15.00 |
| Lipstick Dom **(LGBT)** | _____ | $15.00 |
| A School of Dolls **(LGBT)** | _____ | $15.00 |
| Hoetic Justice | _____ | $15.00 |
| KALI: Raunchy Relived | _____ | $15.00 |
| (5<sup>th</sup> Book in Raunchy Series) | | |
| Skeezers | _____ | $15.00 |
| Skeezers 2 | _____ | $15.00 |
| You Kissed Me, Now I Own You | _____ | $15.00 |
| Nefarious | _____ | $15.00 |
| Redbone 3: The Rise of The Fold | _____ | $15.00 |
| The Fold (4<sup>th</sup> Redbone Book) _____ | | $15.00 |
| Clown Niggas | _____ | $15.00 |
| The One You Shouldn't Trust _____ | | $15.00 |
| The WHORE The Wind | | |
| Blew My Way | _____ | $15.00 |
| She Brings The Worst Kind | _____ | $15.00 |
| The House That Crack Built | _____ | $15.00 |
| The House That Crack Built 2 _____ | | 15.00 |
| The House That Crack Built 3 _____ | | $15.00 |
| The House That Crack Built 4 _____ | | $15.00 |
| Level Up **(LGBT)** | _____ | $15.00 |
| Villains: It's Savage Season | _____ | $15.00 |
| Gay For My Bae | _____ | $15.00 |
| War | _____ | $15.00 |
| War 2: All Hell Breaks Loose | _____ | $15.00 |
| War 3: The Land Of The Lou's | _____ | $15.00 |

**263**

# HERSBAND MATERIAL 2: JAILHOUSE BUTCH

War 4: Skull Island _____ $15.00
War 5: Karma _____ $15.00
War 6: Envy _____ $15.00
War 7: Pink Cotton _____ $15.00
Madjesty vs. Jayden (Novella) _____ $8.99
You Left Me No Choice _____ $15.00
Truce – A War Saga (War 8) _____ $15.00
Ask The Streets For Mercy _____ $15.00
Truce 2 (War 9) _____ $15.00
An Ace and Walid Very, Very Bad Christmas (War 10) ___ $15.00
Truce 3 – The Sins of The Fathers (War 11) _____ $15.00
Truce 4: The Finale (War 12) _____ $15.00
Treason _____ $20.00
Treason 2 _____ $20.00
Hersband Material 2 **(LGBT)** _____ $15.00

**(Redbone 1 & 2 are NOT Cartel Publications novels and if <u>ordered</u> the cost is FULL price of $16.00 each plus shipping. No Exceptions.)**

Please add **$7.00** for shipping and handling fees for up to **(2) BOOKS PER ORDER.** (INMATES INCLUDED) (See next page for details)

## The Cartel Publications * P.O. BOX 486 OWINGS MILLS MD 21117

Name: _____

Address: _____

City/State: _____

Contact/Email: _____

*Please allow 10-15 BUSINESS days Before shipping.*

***PLEASE NOTE DUE TO <u>COVID-19</u> SOME ORDERS MAY TAKE UP TO <u>3 WEEKS</u> OR LONGER BEFORE THEY SHIP***

**The Cartel Publications is <u>NOT</u> responsible for <u>Prison Orders</u> rejected!**

<u>NO RETURNS and NO REFUNDS</u>
<u>NO PERSONAL CHECKS ACCEPTED</u>
<u>STAMPS NO LONGER ACCEPTED</u>

## BY C. WASH

CPSIA information can be obtained
at www.ICGtesting.com
Printed in the USA
LVHW042042280222
712222LV00015B/2012